Love and Death in The British Isles
A Love and Death Mystery & Political Espionage Novel

Volume 24

Hal Graff

Copyright © 2023 **Harold Graff II Publishing**

All rights reserved. No part of this publication may be reproduced, distributed, or transmitted in any form or by any means, including photocopying, recording, or other electronic or mechanical methods, without the prior written permission of the publisher, except in the case of brief quotations embodied in critical reviews and certain other noncommercial uses permitted by copyright law. For permission requests, write to the publisher, addressed "Attention: Book Rights and Permission," at the address below.

Published in the United States of America

ISBN 978-1-962730-77-8 (SC)
ISBN 979-8-89395-925-3 (HC)
ISBN 978-1-962730-54-9 (Ebook)

Harold Graff II Publishing
222 West 6th Street
Suite 400, San Pedro, CA, 90731
sec26para5@yahoo.com

Order Information and Rights Permission:

Quantity sales. Special discounts might be available on quantity purchases by corporations, associations, and others. For details, contact the publisher at the address above.

For Book Rights Adaptation and other Rights Permission. Call us at toll-free 1-888-945-8513 or send us an email at admin@stellarliterary.com.

NOVELS BY DR. HAL GRAFF
(6,478,043 total published words)

The Love and Death Series
Harold Gatewood Mysteries
(Mystery / Political Espionage)

Love and Death at The Encierro Vol. 1
Love and Death in Cuba Vol. 2
Love and Death in Tokyo Vol. 3
Love and Death in Beijing Vol. 4
Love and Death in London Vol. 5
Love and Death in Korea Vol. 6
Love and Death in Venezuela Vol. 7
Love and Death in Mexico Vol. 8
Love and Death in The Dominican Republic Vol. 9
Love and Death: A Journey Vol. 10
Love and Death in Tuscon Vol. 11
The Harold Gatewood Mysteries: An Encyclopedia Vol. 12 (Not Available. For my use only)
Love and Death in Virginia Vol. 13
Love and Death in Chile Vol. 14
Love and Death in Paris Vol.15
Love and Death in The Orient Vol. 16
Love and Death in The China Sea Vol. 17
Love and Death in Caracas Vol. 18
Love and Death in Chicago Vol. 19
Love and Death in Moscow Vol. 20
Love and Death in The Ukraine Vol. 21
Love and Death in Rome Vol. 22
The Harold Gatewood Mysteries: An Encyclopedia Vol. 2 (The encyclopedia is not available. For my use only)
Love and Death in the British Isles Vol. 24
Love and Death in the Philippines Vol. 25
Love and Death in Barcelona Vol. 26
Gatewood Returns Vol. 27

The Davis Finn Mysteries
(Historical Fiction / Mystery Thrillers / Political Espionage)

Murder in Georgia Vol. 1 (A Quadrillage – Book 1)
Murder in Montana Vol. 2 (A Quadrillage - Book 2)
Murder in The FBI Vol. 3 (A Quadrillage – Book 3)
Murder in Vietnam Vol. 4 (A Quadrillage – Book 4)
Angel of Mercy Vol. 5
Oxy Vol. 6 (A Trilogy – Book 1)
The White Duck Vol. 7 (A Trilogy – Book 2)
Sucker Punch Vol. 8 (A Trilogy – Book 3)
Eddy Vol. 9
Counterfeit Vol. 10 (A Trilogy – Book 1)
Montenegro Vol. 11 (A Trilogy – Book 2)
Triple Crown Vol. 12 (A Trilogy – Book 3)
Murder in Oxford Vol. 13 (A Trilogy – Book 1)
Revenge Vol. 14 (A Trilogy – Book 2)
Survival Vol. 15 (A Trilogy – Book 3)
The Mississippi Hangman Vol. 16 (A Trilogy – Book 1)
A Dead President Vol. 17 (A Trilogy – Book 2)
Oath of Office Vol. 18 (A Trilogy – Book 3)
Finn and Gatewood's Outdoor Adventures Vol. 19
Stockholm Syndrome Vol. 20 (A Trilogy – Book 1)
Blood Feud Vol. 21 (A Trilogy – Book 2)
A Terrible Tragedy Vol. 22 (A Trilogy – Book 3)
Takedown Vol.23
Blackmail Vol. 24
Dead Like Lincoln Vol. 25
Lethal Force Vol. 26
The Leopard Vol. 27
The Crossbow Killer Vol. 28
The Ten Pin Killer Vol. 29
The Grand Bargain Vol. 30
Jill Vol. 31 (A Trilogy – Book 1)
Double-cross Vol. 32 (A Trilogy – Book 2)
The Seven Iron Murders Vol.33 (A Trilogy – Book 3)
The Corner Pocket Killer Vol. 34
The Credit Card Murders Vol 35
The Choke Hold Murders Vol. 36
The Midterm Elections Vol. 37
Death Dressed in Blue Vol. 38

His Better Half Vol. 39
Ten Little Indians Vol. 40 (A Trilogy – Book 1)
The Cassowary Vol. 41 (A Trilogy – Book 2)
Remember, Remember, The 5th Of November Vol. 42 (A Trilogy – Book 3)

The Parker Weston Romance Mysteries

Penelope Vol. 1 (A Trilogy – Book 1)
The Bad Boy Vol. 2 (A Trilogy – Book 2)
Tall Buffalo Vol. 3 (A Trilogy – Book 3)
1, 2, 3, 4, Enter Murder's Door Vol. 4 (A Trilogy – Book 1)
The Sky's The Limit, John Vol. 5 (A Trilogy – Book 2)
Love Will Keep Us Together Vol. 6 (A Trilogy – Book 3)

The Bobby Ross Faith Series

Bobby Ross And the White Stones Vol. 1

The Aidan Conall Mysteries

Carnage At Harvard Vol. 1 (A Trilogy – Book 1)
Its Forty – Love Vol. 2 (A Trilogy – Book 2)
Its Match Point Vol. 3 (A Trilogy – Book 3)

The Wes Oakley Action, Adventure Series

Assassination In Ketchum Vol. 1 (Of A Duology)
Revenge on the Mountain Vol. 2 (Of A Duology)
Bad Medicine Vol. 3 (A Trilogy – Book 1)
Smuggler Vol. 4 (A Trilogy – Book 2)
Beauty Queen Vol. 5 (A Trilogy – Book 3)
Stick 'em Up, Pardner Vol. 6
The 8 Second Killer Vol. 7
9! 10! It's Over! Vol. 8
Now You See Her Vol. 9
The Golden Boy Vol. 10
Bodies In Barrels Vol. 11
A Ten Pounder Vol. 12 (A Trilogy - Book 1)
The Disappearance Vol. 13 (A Trilogy – Book 2)
Try, Try. Try Again Vol. 14 (A Trilogy – Book 3)

For Eric, Lainen, Colton, Ethan, Jenny, Scott, Finn, and Kade

And for my Creator, my God in Heaven, my Lord and Savior, Jesus Christ, my comforter, and guide, the Holy Spirit, and the Holy Trinity

Disclaimer

This story is a work of fiction. The names of characters, their actions, locations, events, situations, organizations, companies, religious or ethnic groups, story line, and any other item in this fictional work are the result of my creation. Any likeness to the areas mentioned above, or people living, or who have passed away, is accidental and was not used for any harmful purpose in this work of fiction.

Table of Contents

Prologue xi
Chapter 1 A Welcome Guest 1
Chapter 2 Surprise, Surprise 23
Chapter 3 "All we can get" 26
Chapter 4 "It is nice to meet you." 34
Chapter 5 The World Goes On 38
Chapter 6 Afghanistan 43
Chapter 7 Columbia, South Carolina 47
Chapter 8 The Philippines 51
Chapter 9 IOFFI 55
Chapter 10 WISAM 58
Chapter 11 SPFIF 60
Chapter 12 Set To Explode 63
Chapter 13 Talpidae 74
Chapter 14 To London 77
Chapter 15 OWFA 80
Chapter 16 "I miss him" 82
Chapter17 North Male Atoll, Maldives 84
Chapter 18 To Ireland 87
Chapter 19 On To Scotland 93
Chapter 20 On To Wales 96
Chapter 21 Boom 98
Chapter 22 To London 101
Chapter 23 The Prime Minister 105
Chapter 24 The Head of National Security 109
Chapter 25 A Knockout 111
Chapter 26 Progress 113
Chapter 27 At The Masque 116
Chapter 28 From Damascus 118
Chapter 29 Ready, Set… 121
Chapter 30 Catching Up 124
Chapter 31 Go… 126
Chapter 32 D.C. 129

Prologue

THE MISSION IN ROME HAD ENDED IN A DAZE FOR Gatewood, as he had no recollection of how he had found himself lying next to a corpse in the catacombs of Rome. The last few days of his time in Italy had seen sudden and dramatic changes, and had opened up new threats to American interests in Europe.

Gatewood had found a new love in Gianna Sabina, and both had been enjoying their time together. He had been involved in what had been a relaxed mission, free of danger, until early-December.

In America, Gatewood's parents had celebrated Thanksgiving, had started to prepare for the Christmas celebration, and had wondered if their son was alive and well in Italy. They did not know that he and Gianna had celebrated the American holiday in Italian style, eating not turkey, but their favorite Italian meal at their regular restaurant of choice. Afterwards, they had gone to her apartment, made love, and slept until morning when booth of them headed to work.

Gatewood was back on duty, and as usual, Durante and Morte Improvvisa had returned to the papal residence, then entered, for a half-hour meeting, then departed. Harold had known that something other than a discussion about splitting up the proceeds from boats loaded with of illegal immigrants was in play.

The next day, he had watched as the scene repeated itself. He had then relaxed assuming that nothing else was going to happen for thirty minute when Durante and Improvvisa would reappear, and then depart for the day.

As he waited, he had thought about the date, December seventh, nineteen-forty-one, the day that the Japanese forces bombed American's naval fleet in Honolulu, Hawaii. The result had been that America entered World War II, defeated Adolf Hitler's Germany, and helped change the course of human history. He had hoped that a current catastrophe would not take place on his mission in Rome.

He had headed to the bathroom, washed his face with cold water, looked in the mirror and saw face, tired from days of glassing the Vatican courtyard. He had thrown the towel on the counter, and a twinge of pain had run through his right arm up and into the socket where his shoulder joined is torso.

His broken-down arm and shoulder, victims of years of throwing baseballs, enduring surgeries, and surviving a rifle shot from ex, now-deceased AIO National Commander Ekain Koldo, was ruined. He had looked in the mirror and said, "Thank you Susana Richards for killing Koldo. I love you." He then returned to glass the expected exit by Durante and Improvvisa.

The thirty minutes had then passed, and the anticipated departure had not taken place. Unexpectedly, a new figure had approached the papal residence. It was Natalio Vicent, leader of the TCPLM in Caracas, Venezuela. Gatewood had wondered why Vicent was there.

Then, two more figures, Rafael and Edwardo Carmelo, had approached, and entered the papal residence. Whatever was happening was big, much more than the sharing of boat people money. Gatewood had remained glued to his viewing spot for over an hour until, one-by-one, Vicent and the Carmelo Brothers, had exited and left the Vatican grounds.

After the cartel members had departed, Gatewood called Rick Owens to report his findings and ask for additional instructions. He had known that no matter what Owens said, he was going to remain at his post, as he was going to find out what unlawful actions were being planned.

Owens had told Harold to remain at his post, and keep him informed of the daily developments. He had also said, "Be careful Harold. There are dangerous people gathering in Rome. People who want to kill you."

After thinking about the situation, and formulating a plan, Gatewood had then called Gianna, asked her to spend the night with him, and showered. When she arrived, he kissed her, and then suggested they go to supper. When they returned to the room for the night, they had made love, and talked.

He had trouble concentrating on their conversation, a fact which Gianna had noticed. "Harold, you are distracted. What has happened?"

"There was an interesting development in my work today." He had then told her that a group of businessmen he had been instructed to monitor had showed up unexpectedly, and his assignment duties were going to have to be changed. "It is nothing that I can't adjust to, but I have a lot of work ahead of me."

She said she understood, but he had barely heard her words. He was thinking, "All but one."

The situation repeated itself over the next two days, as Gatewood had watched the participants gather at the same time, enter the papal residence, have their meeting, exit into the courtyard, and then leave. He had patiently waited for something to happen to break what he sensed was a stalemate in the group's discussions.

The wild card that would break the stalemate then arrived quickly. On December eleventh, Harold had watched the cartel and mafia figures arrive. First were Durante and Improvvisa, followed by Vicent, and then the Carmelo brothers. They had broken tradition, and did not enter the residence, instead taking seats on the benches in the courtyard.

Gatewood had thought, "What is happening?"

His question was soon answered. His eyes almost jumped out of his eyes as he saw a new figure approach the group. Traditional mafia-style hugs were then exchanged, followed by handshakes, slaps on the back, smiles, and laughter. He had been able to use his lip-reading skills and made out that this latest figure was the man who would break the stalemate in the discussions.

Gatewood had then screamed, "Dam you Masas!"

The man who had arrived was Salvator Masas, the "El Avispon Picante", the "Stinging Hornet". He had traveled from Mexico to join in the discussions. Gatewood's blood boiled with anger as he watched his number one enemy smile and laugh with his drug-pushing cartel buddies.

Harold had despised Masas for contributing to the deaths of three wonderful women he had loved, Jeong Eun, the beautiful North Korean who had become his lover in Cabo San Lucas, Mexico, Ju Won, his gorgeous mistress from North Korea who had disappeared in the South China Sea, floating away from him never to be seen again, and a woman he had loved deeply, Luisa Gaicia, who had been killed in Gibson City, Illinois.

He had watched the group of evil cartel thugs enter the papal residence and thought that they were discussing how to increase the number of illegal immigrants in Europe and the United States. Doing so would lead to more payments to the Catholic Church from the World United Community, the organization that promoted peace and cooperation between countries.

He had also thought that plans were being hatched to not only increase the church's take of the fees extracted from the illegal immigrants for their passage to Italy, but to also share the fees the cartels would gather from the illegals for providing drugs and prostitution services. The deal would result in a disgusting, dirty, amoral association that would make the cartels, and the church outrageously wealthy. He had waited, watched, and thought about what to do. He had then decided to go to the street across from the entry gate of Vatican City and wait.

After arriving he took sat down on a bench out of the sight of people leaving the Vatican grounds, and waited for the cartel leaders to leave. First, Vicent had appeared, then walked away toward his safe house. He was followed by the Carmelo brothers, who did the same as Vicent.

Next to appear was Fabbri Durante and Improvvisa, who turned right and started to walk away. Gatewood thought that he had been spotted by Improvvisa, who whispered something to Durante. Neither man had looked in Gatewood's direction, and continued walking. That left only one person, "The Big Fish", the man Gatewood had decided to follow, Salvador Masas.

"The Hornet" had then appeared, turned left, and started to walk away. Gatewood had stayed on the other side of the street from Masas, and started to tail him, always staying close behind, but out of sight.

The cat-and-mouse drama had continued to unfold, with the target stopping to look in several storefronts to window shop. Gatewood had not seen Masas turn around, and hoped that his reflection had not been spotted in the storefront windows. Even if it had, Gatewood was committed to following, catching, terrorizing and extracting information about the mission from Masas about the unholy alliance the group had struck with the Pope. Then, he would kill "The Hornet" for his role in Jeong Eng, Ju Won, and Luisa Gaicia's deaths.

Masas continued to walk, had then entered the catacombs, and descended to the area below the streets of Rome. Gatewood had followed, and slowly walked through the maze of tunnels and rooms in the dark, musty catacombs, to find Masas.

As Harold had passed each opening, tunnel, and passageway, he had looked to his right, then left, and then continued to proceed on ahead. As he had reached the next tunnel, he had glanced to his left, and had then been thrown to the ground as Masas, a burly man, had plowed into him as if he were a running back crossing the goal line to win the Super Bowl. Both men had then fallen to the ground, then gotten up, and started a battle that both of them wanted to end in death, as their hatred of each other had been boiling over for years.

Harold had turned to face his enemy just in time to see an overhead, downward thrust of Masas's right hand heading downward toward his shoulder and head. Harold's taekwondo lessons paid off again as he reacted with a rising block, a chookya makgi, of the blow with the right underside of his forearm absorbing the force of his enemy's thrust. Gatewood had then attacked with a spring hook kick, finding the flab of Masas' stomach, and sending him backward toward the catacomb's sediment-laden walls.

Masas then regained his balance, and had charged Gatewood, propelling both of them into the opposite wall of the chamber. Gatewood's head had crashed into the wall, causing him to become dizzy. The attacker had again rushed toward him to fulfill the Hornet's mission of terminating his nemesis.

Harold had regained his balance, arisen to a position where he was still on the ground but sitting up, reached under the bulge of his long-sleeve shirt, and had withdrawn a pistol. Before he could fire, Masas had knocked the pistol from his hand. Masas had then thrust his right arm and fist downward toward Harold's face, which Harold dodged. Harold then stood up and faced his attacker again.

Masas had then attacked, and landed a three-hundred-sixty degree tornado kick. Harold then raised his arms into Taekwondo fighting position and was able to pare off a hand thrust at his head. A roundhouse kick by his attacker had been stopped with a blocking movement with his right forearm. The two figures had then faced each other again, with the same thought in mind, to kill the man opposite them.

Hand-to-hand combat had again continued, with each man landing combinations of closed and open-hand attacks performed from standing, jumping, spinning, and rushing positions.

Then, Masas again grabbed Harold and both men then fell to the dirt. As they wrestled, Harold had tasted the dirt as it entered his mouth, and started to choke as the dust from the dirt started to fill his lungs.

Gatewood had then rolled over, gained the advantage, and found himself on top of Masas, choking him with both hands. His grip then became tighter and tighter, as his enemy tried to free himself form Harold's choke hold. As Harold had gripped the man's throat he felt rage and hatred for Masas, who now deserved all the punishment he was dishing out.

Harold had seen the life start to disappear from the man's eyes, and had increased his choking action with all of his strength. The man's resistance had then grown weaker and weaker. Harold had known what the man was thinking, as he had experienced it himself when AIO agent Eneko Itzal had tried to strangle him in the park in Beijing, China.

The stages of death that Harold had experienced were now taking the man along death's path. He was choking. Masas had then experienced shortness of breath, panicked, struggled and displayed desperate actions to free himself from the death grip. He had then advanced toward the act of passing out, the next step in his journey into death's dark channel.

Gatewood had almost sent Masas to hades went he felt the pain of a crashing blow to his skull. He then fell backwards, and before starting to pass into unconsciousness, had seen Masas stand up, look at him, then walk away. Harold had then passed out.

When Gatewood had again come to his senses, he had struggled to his feet, tried to gain his bearings, and then looked around. To his right, Morte Improvvisa, Fabbri Durante's mafia assassin, laid dead on his right side, in the dirt. He had been shot from behind, and blood had flowed from its exit wound in the victim's chest on to the dirt near the body.

Gatewood had wondered, "How did he get here?" He had then realized that the assassin had circled back to follow him after he and Durante had walked away in an opposite direction of Harold's tail on Masas.

More questions had then flooded Harold's mind. "Who shot him? "Why was he shot?" "Who had something to gain if Improvvisa was killed?"

Realizing that he may now be in danger, he had fled to his hotel, called Rick Owens, and reported what had happened. He had then asked Owens what he should do, and was advised to go to the American embassy in Rome, stay there, and that he would soon be taken out of Rome and flown back to America. He would then be free of an Italian police investigation, and would be flown back to Washington for debriefing.

When he was safely sequestered in the embassy, he had called Gianna. There had been no answer. Over the next twenty-four hours he had tried repeatedly to contact her. He had called her cell number, her landlord, and the tour company where she worked. All efforts had drawn a blank.

He had become despondent, as he wanted to talk with her. Where was she? Had she left Rome? Had she left Italy? Had something sinister happened to her?

He was then escorted to the airport and placed on an American government, CIO airplane, and flown back to Washington. Harold's mind had struggled to find the answers, but none were available, as Gianna Sabina had vanished into thin air.

In Argentina, the National Commander of the OWFLA, Aldofito Imanol, had made a call on his cell phone. "Gianna, this is Imanol. I wanted to personally thank you for your fine work in Rome. Your killing of Morte Improvvisa was a stroke of brilliance as it will further create unrest in the citizens of Italy, knowing that America has been sending their agent Harold Gatewood to kill Italian citizens.

It will also create more disdain in the world for America, making our mission to install a one world government for all much easier. We are going to call on you in the future, as no doubt Gatewood will be sent to foil our efforts again soon, and you will be once again be able to use him to further our organization's mission."

Gianna Sabina had listened intently to Imanol's comments, and had responded "Thank you" at the end of the conversation. She was a believer in the OWFA's cause, but she had not killed Morte Improvvisa for the good of the organization. She had done so because she loved Gatewood, and Improvvisa was going to kill her lover at Fabbri Durante's orders.

A tear had then rolled down Gianna's cheek, and she had said, "I love you Harold, and no one is going to kill you if I can help it."

Chapter 1

A Welcome Guest

December 25

AFTER CELEBRATING CHRISTMAS WITH HIS PARENTS, Gatewood helped his dad and mom take down the Christmas tree and decorations, pack them in boxes, and take them to the basement storage room until next year. He then talked with his parents, and thanked God for how blessed his life had been, and asked that his good fortune continue.

On the twenty-sixth, his parents left for Ft. Myers, Florida to spend the Winter basking in the sun, and playing golf. The next day Susana Richards flew in to spend a week with Harold, as was becoming her habit. She was in between contract killings and the couple had promised to pamper each other until she had to fly to home to finish her preparation for her assignment.

After doing his morning workout, Gatewood headed out the front door for a brisk hour's walk in the cold December air. As he breathed the cold air into his lungs and exhaled, his breath filled the atmosphere with puffs of smoke. It was much colder than he liked, but being outside in the twenty-degree air gave him time to think.

He still thought of Gianna and wondered what had become of her. She had disappeared, and he had come to the realization that she might never reappear in his life. He decided to put her out of his thoughts, because alive or dead, she was an unanswered question in his life. And, he was anxious to be with Susana again.

After showering, he headed to Bloomington to the Central Illinois Airport to wait for Susana. He watched her, smiling from ear-to-ear, walk from the plane toward him. He smiled back, realizing that she was even more beautiful today than any other time he had ever seen her.

They kissed, and started to talk as they made their way to the baggage claim area. She continued to smile, and looked him in the eyes, held his hand, and draped her left arm around his waist, as she talked. He had never seen her as loving and affectionate in public as she was today.

After retrieving her suitcase, she followed him to the car, and held his hand as he drove the thirty-five miles to his home. After arriving, she immediately led him to the bedroom and made love to him over and over again. Exhausted, they both dozed off to sleep after talking for an hour. When they awoke they showered together, and fixed supper.

The process continued for five days, and the couple seemed closer than they had ever been. When they went to sleep that night, Harold had a dream. He vividly recalled the first time they had ever spoken.

Years ago, before he had gone to Mexico to scout for baseball prospects, and before he had found Luisa Gaicia alive in Mexico City, he had been relaxing after his workouts and considering fixing himself a salad of spinach leaves, mixed greens, carrots, onions, green, red, and yellow peppers, garbanzo beans, green peas, peanuts, corn, and sunflower seeds, when his cell phone rang.

He had looked at the number and realized it was the same one he had seen three times in the past week. Each time, a short message had been left. This time, he hoped to talk to the calling party. He remembered the conversation, word for word.

"Hi, this is Harold Gatewood."

"Oh my, I am so excited that I have finally caught you."

He laughed and said, "Caught me? That would be a good trick."

The female voice on the phone tried to gather her composure. Finally, she introduced myself. "Harold this is your biggest fan."

"Hi biggest fan. What is your name?"

"Susanna."

"Susanna who?"

"Susanna Richards."

"Do we have the pleasure of knowing each other yet"

"No, not yet."

"How can I help you Susanna?"

"I am the head of the Harold Gatewood fan club."

"Really. I didn't know I had one."

"Oh yes. I have followed your career, and your exciting life."

"Well thank you. How can I help you."

"I live in Northern Minnesota, ten miles from Ontario, Canada."

"What town?"

"I live in Scalp, Minnesota."

"That is an unusual name for a town."

"Yes, we get teased about it all the time."

"Susanna, what can I do for you?"

"I wanted to invite you to Scalp, Minnesota for the first annual Harold Gatewood Fan Club celebration and the first Harold Gatewood Hero Recognition Day this Fall."

"Are you putting me on Susanna?"

"No. I am serious. I am always serious about you Harold."

"Well, thanks for the invitation, but I am afraid I can't make it."

"Please Harold, can you come? I will make it worth your while."

"Thanks anyway Susanna. I wish you well."

"Harold, you need to come to Scalp to see the celebration. It will be a wonderful event, especially if you come. I would like you to deliver a speech about your career."

"I am sorry Susanna but I don't give speeches."

"Harold, can I send you some information about the celebration, and your fan club?"

"Sure."

"I know you live in Gibson City, Illinois. Can I have your address?"

"I don't give that information out to anyone."

"If I send the packet to Gibson City will it be delivered to you?"

"I think so."

"Okay. I will. Harold, I have a question for you?"

"Have you signed a contract to play baseball this year?"

"No."

"What are you going to do?"

"I am going to get well and recover from my surgery. These questions are too personal. Is there anything else?"

"Can I interview you?"

"I don't know you."

"We can correct that Harold."

"Susanna, I appreciated your call but I need to go."

"Okay. Thank you for listening about the celebration. I am sorry you can't come as it would be nice to meet you."

"Thank you. Good luck."

"Thank you Harold."

Gatewood hung up the phone and thought, "What a ridiculous call. Scalp, Minnesota. I am going to look that town up to see if it really exists."

He walked into his office, grabbed his world atlas, and thumbed through the alphabetical listing of towns in the world. Sure enough, Scalp, Minnesota was listed. Harold laughed loudly when he read the population figure for the town. It was 143 people, total.

He continued laughing for five minutes, being ashamed but amused that he had fallen for such a prank call. He wondered which of his friends had put Susanna Richards, if that was her name, up to doing that.

In Scalp, Minnesota, Susanna Richards put her cell phone down on her desk, stood up, and looked at herself in the full length mirror in her bedroom. She liked what she saw.

She was five-feet-seven-inches tall, with long black hair that stopped at the top of her tailbone, beautiful black eyelashes, dazzling brown "bedroom" eyes, a perfectly-shaped mouth, luscious lips, pearly-white, perfectly-formed teeth, a perfect Fibonacci ratio, magnificent breasts, and a perfect .7 waist to hip ratio. She weighed one hundred and ten pounds, all of which were perfectly proportioned on her gorgeous body.

She smiled and thought, "You may not know me now Harold Gatewood, but you will soon. And, you will always remember me. We will meet, I will catch you, and you will love me. You will be mine Harold Gatewood"

Little did Harold know that Susan was going to enter his life like a tornado, and change it forever. She would become obsessed with him, and kill the CEO Gerald Andersen, Vice-President of Operations Grady Elliott, and Senior Marketing Representative Loren Melnor of the Placer de los Lectores book company for cheating him out of his book royalties.

She would also become his hated enemy for killing his lover, Luisa Gaicia, whom he had me and fallen in love with in Venezuela. He remembered the horrifying details of Susana's actions.

Harold and Luisa left Mexico City for Illinois on March sixteenth. They arrived in Chicago, then had flown to the Bloomington airport, where Harold's parents picked them up and drove them to Gibson City.

After spending time together and getting to know each other each other, Harold and Luisa went to his home. After relaxing, and making love, they slept soundly until the next morning. Harold's mother and Luisa would spend time working on crafts, and Harold and his dad would talk about the farm business until evening. After supper Luisa told Harold she would like to take a walk by herself as she wanted to think about how she could do something wonderful for his parents, as they had treated her so nicely and had graciously accepted her.

Forty-five minutes stretched into an hour and a half, and then into two and a half hours, and Luisa had not returned. Harold had become concerned that she might have been hit by a car as she walked on the country road in front of his house. He decided to wait ten more minutes before driving North to find her. He anxiously answered his phone when it rang, as he expected she was on her was back to the house.

"Harold, this is Susana."

"Susana, I am surprised to hear from you."

"You did not tell me you were coming back home Harold."

"I left in a hurry."

"I told you to always let me know of your whereabouts honey."

"I am sorry. Where are you?"

"I am close to you honey. I always want to be close to you."

"That is nice Susana, but where are you?"

"I am less than a mile from you."

"A mile? Are you in Gibson City?"

"Yes."

"How did you get here?"

"I drove here, and have been waiting for you honey."

"I thought you were in New York City."

"Oh, New York City. Yes, I was there for a while."

"What happened there?"

"I had to correct a situation at the Placer de los Lectores book publishing company for you."

"What did you do?"

"I took tribal vengeance on the three men who insulted your honor in print, and made them regret their cruel and disdainful misdeeds."

"Susana, did you kill those three men?"

"Yes. I killed Atkinson first. Then I killed Elliott in a similar manner. And, I saved the best until last. I killed Melnor as the grand finale because he mistreated you in person."

"How could you torture, scalp, and mutilate them?"

"The acts of revenge were needed to wash away the lies they printed about you."

"That was cruel."

"No, it was revenge, and justice."

"How long have you been here?"

"I have been scouting the area for three days."

"Scouting for what?"

"For the perfect place of course."

"Perfect place for what?"

"The perfect place to separate Luisa from your life."

"What?"

"The perfect place to make sure Luisa exits your life."

"You can't do that."

"Of course I can. It is our destiny."

"There is no destiny for you and I."

"Oh yes Harold. We will be together forever."

"No we won't."

"Harold, you need to let me take care of things and then we can be together."

"I want to come to where you are."

"Good. I want you to watch things play out."

"Where are you?"

"I am at the scene where many of your talents got a start, and where you had many nice moments."

"Where is that?"

"Go to the high school and park in the lot behind the boy's locker room. Walk across the street, then enter the baseball diamond. Walk in from the outfield and stop at home plate. Remain there until you hear from me. Do not leave the home plate area."

"Alright."

Once he reached the school, he did as he was instructed. He stood at home plate and looked in horror at the backstop. Luisa was tied to the wire screen. Her arms were outstretched and her legs were bound together. She was tied in a manner of a person being crucified on a cross. Her head was hanging down, her chin on her chest. He called her name and she raised her head, and looked at him, her eyes begging for help. She had been beaten. Blood had dried on her face, near her nostrils.

Harold's phone rang, and a voice said, "There she is, in all of her glory. Luisa and I had a nice conversation. Eventually, she saw things my way and agreed to be here like this, waiting for you."

Harold looked around. He scanned the bleachers and area behind the backstop. He then looked at track area behind the dugouts. No one was in the area. He wanted to go to Luisa but dared not do so as he had been warned to stay put.

"Harold, how do you like how Luisa looks now?"

"You are very cruel Susana."

"Perhaps Harold. But, I wanted to get your attention."

"You have. Let her go."

"No, she must pay for making you chase all over Mexico to find her."

"Please, let her go."

"I think not my love."

"Can I go to the fence to talk to her?"

"Yes, I want you to do that."

Harold walked to the fence, hugged Luisa as best as he cold, and spoke softly to her. "It will be fine honey. I am here."

Susana's voice came over a speaker that was located nearby. "That was very touching Harold. But, that is not going to happen. Kiss her."

Harold did as ordered. He kissed her, wiped the dried blood from her nose, and told her that he was going to free her. A voice was heard again, "Yes Harold, I want you to hold her."

Harold quickly untied the ropes that bound Luisa to the wire of the backstop and held her in his arms. She meekly kissed him, as she was exhausted physically. He returned the kiss and told her things were going to be alright.

Susana's voice was then heard. "Kiss her one more time Harold."

He kissed Luisa and told her he loved her. Susana's voice was again heard. "That was your goodbye kiss." A rifle shot raced through the air, and entered Luisa's head, splattering blood, bone, and brain tissue on Harold's face, arms, and hands.

Luisa's body went limp, and Harold, holding her in his arms, slumped to the ground. He held her lifeless body to his chest and started to sob. They both had made long journeys to be together again. It was not right their future together would end like this, her dead in his arms, both sitting on the ground by the backstop.

Harold heard a car engine start, looked at the far end of the football field, and saw a car speed away, North from Gibson City. Susana's voice was again heard on the speaker, "I will see you soon Harold."

She had caused him much grief, and he had hated her for a long time for her act of killing Luisa. He had continued to try to resume his baseball career, and had helped the CIO in the Dominican Republic. He had put Susana out of his mind as he flew to the island to even the score with the Columbian and Venezuelan drug cartels. He did not know that she would reappear in his life. He thought about the incident, recalling the details explicitly.

He had walked from his mailbox by the road back to his front door. On the way he opened a letter that was adorned with the smell of a woman's perfume. He turned the key in his door lock and walked to his kitchen table.

He sat down and opened the aromatically-induced envelope and glanced at the single sentence typed in the middle of the page. It read:

My darling, please join me in Santo Domingo, in the Dominican Republic.
Love,
Susanna

Gatewood read the letter three times, gathered his thoughts, and placed the single sheet of paper on the kitchen table, and said, "The Dominican Republic. What an unusual and, unpleasant, coincidence. I wonder what Susana is up to now."

He sipped his hot chocolate, finished his oatmeal, and headed to the workout building behind the house. He progressed through his stretching, tai chi, taekwondo and Brazilian jiu-jitsu drills and started is transcendental meditation session. He soon realized that his breathing and relaxation exercise was to no avail, as he could not get the letter out of his mind.

He next moved to his hitting drills. As he hit one baseball after another off the batting tee and into the net, he realized that the session was not going to be beneficial as long as he was thinking about Susana Richards. He threw in the towel on the morning workout and headed back to the house.

He grabbed a glass of ice water and headed to the chair by the window in the living room. He looked at his loyal friends, the birds and the squirrels, and picked up three pieces of typing paper and a pen that was on the end table near him.

He thought for several moments about the situation and then reached for his cell phone to make a call to his parents. He discussed the letter with his dad and mom and then outlined his plans for their safety, and his reaction to the "call for a pow wow" with Susana. All three came to a like-minded result.

Gatewood then hung up, and dialed a second number. He was greeted by a pleasant female voice.

"Hello, this is the CIO."
"Hi. May I please speak with Rick Owens?"
"What is your name Sir?"
"Harold Gatewood."
"One moment please."
He was then connected to his friend and former employer.
"Hello Harold. How are you?"
"Hi Rick. I am doing pretty well."
"What is on your mind this morning Harold?"
"I received a letter this morning from our friend Susana Richards,"
"What did it say?"
Harold read the note and asked Rick for his opinion on its contents.
"She could just be baiting you. Or, ..."
"Or what Rick?"

"Or she means what she wrote."

"What are your thoughts?"

"It is too important a possibility to ignore."

Harold then spoke, "I think I should go there. I have made arrangements to have a bodyguard watch my parents while I go to Santo Domingo. I will only be gone a week or two."

He then boarded a plane for his trip to Santiago. On board, he put down his tourist guidebook and closed his eyes for a short nap. He was tired. When he awoke he noticed the woman in the seat next to him still working diligently on her pile of legal papers.

He looked at her purse, which was sitting on the floor by her feet and below the seat in the row in front of her. He noticed an Arizona driver's license. He tried not to be obvious but he failed.

While it sounded impossible to him since he was a fan of beautiful women, he had not noticed that she was gorgeous. She had short blonde hair, wide blue eyes, high cheekbones, and a nice trio of a beautiful mouth, straight teeth, and luscious lips.

She was dressed in a conservative charcoal-gray colored business suit, a white blouse buttoned at the top that hid what Gatewood surmised to be a wonderful build, and a pair of black, one-inch heeled shoes.

She did not wear a wedding ring but had a turquoise-colored ring on the pinkie finger of her left hand.

She looked up and caught him checking her out. She smiled, her eyes twinkled, and she subconsciously licked her lips with her tongue. She then returned to her work.

Gatewood flagged down the flight attendant and asked if he could have a glass of ice water, which was immediately delivered. He then said, "I am sorry Miss. I should have asked you if you wanted anything to drink when I had the flight attendant bring me this

water."

She answered. "No thank you. I do not want anything at this time."

Since it was obvious that she was not interested in talking to him at this time, he relaxed in his seat, and did not speak for ten minutes. She suddenly put her papers away in her folder and placed them in her briefcase, which she then placed on the floor next to her purse.

She took off her glasses and looked at Gatewood. A smile crept from the corners of her mouth and she said, "Thank you. That was very kind of you to think of me when your water was delivered by the flight attendant."

Harold smiled and said, "You're welcome. Would you like something to drink now? You have been working very hard."

"Yes, I would."

Gatewood hit the call button for the flight attendant and asked the woman what she would like to drink.

She replied, "A glass of water would be nice."

When the flight attendant arrived he ordered a water for his row companion and asked her a question. "What kind of work do you do?"

"International law."

"Where do you practice?"

"My firm is in Portland, Maine. I travel. My main clients are in Madrid, Spain, Rome, Italy, Mexico City, Mexico, London, England, and Santo Domingo, in the Dominican Republic."

"Do you live in Portland?"

"No I live in what is known as the down east part of Maine. The town is called Brunswick."

"Then you live in the same town as the famous Civil War hero, Joshua Chamberlin. Have you gone to his museum?"

"Yes. I am so surprised that you know that fact."

"If you want to know anything obscure, insignificant and unimportant, I am your man."

She laughed and said, "I like you. You are very funny."

"Where did you go to law school?"

"The school is called the Southeastern Diablo Law School, in Phoenix, Arizona."

"Phoenix is almost in the middle of the state."

She laughed and said, "Correct. They were confused about their directions when they named the school."

Gatewood then understood the Arizona driver's license. "That is a long way from Maine. How did you get into law school in Arizona?"

She laughed and said, "I was living in Arizona at the time. I noticed you were looking at a picture of a beautiful lady who was pictured as the screenshot on your computer."

Harold laughed and said, "You are very observant."

She giggled and asked, "Is that your wife?"

"No."

"A girlfriend?"

"Yes, she used to be."

"I am sorry you two broke up. You looked like a nice couple."

"Thanks. We didn't breakup. She was murdered."

She touched his hand and held on to it for a long time before speaking. "I am sorry for your loss. Are you alright?"

"Thanks. I am doing better."

"When did it happen?"

"A few months ago."
"Oh my. How did it happen?"
"She was shot."
"Did they catch the man who shot her?"
"She was shot by a woman."
"Did they catch her?"
"No, not yet."
"I am sorry. Do these questions bother you?"
"No."
"Do you think you will ever love someone else someday?"
"I don't know."
"Have you been to Santo Domingo many times?'
"Yes, many times."
"Do you give guided tours of the city?"
"Yes, but only for very special people."
"Would you show me around Santo Domingo?"
"How long are you going to be here?"
"I will be there through mid-December."
"Unless I am sent back for an emergency to one of my other client accounts I will be there through the end of the year also."

Gatewood asked, "Where are you staying?"
"The La Magnifica Torre, the magnificent tower."
Gatewood said, "That is where I am staying also."

They both laughed and continued to talk until the flight was heading to the runway.

Harold said, "Can I call you for a tour?"
"Of course."

They traded business cards. Her name was Linda Westmorland.

Harold said, "I would have bowed when I gave you the card but I was strapped in the seat for landing."

"I would have curtsied but I was strapped in also."

They landed and bid farewell. When she left she had grabbed Harold's hand, squeezed it tightly, and said, "It was nice to meet Harold. Please call me."

She then leaned in and kissed him gently on the lips, and then walked out of the terminal.

Harold watched her walk away, grabbed his luggage, walked out into the warm Dominican Republic sunshine and said, "I might like the Dominican Republic after all."

The next day he had called her for a date. He had no idea it would lead to the first time they made love, and to the follow-up events that would change his life.

He knocked on the door of her room, six hundred and seven, and waited for Linda Westmorland to welcome him for their date. He had looked forward all day to their being together. Even while he was strolling the streets, watching the men play dominoes, listening to the locales talk baseball at the barber shop, and talking with the voodoo lady, his thoughts were still on Linda.

She opened the door and smiled. She was dressed in a pale blue dress that stopped at her shoulders, had long earrings that drooped two inches below her ear lobes, and wore a matching light-pale-blue ribbon in her hair. She wore light-blue shoes with one inch heels. Harold's eyes followed her legs up from her shoes and to the bottom of her dress, which stopped two inches above her knees.

He then looked at Linda and said, "Wow! You look great."

Harold's unexpected shout of approval startled Linda but she soon broke out into laughter as she realized, one, that he did it to make her relax and laugh, and two, he meant it, as she could tell from his smile and his eyes. She threw her arms around Gatewood's neck, hugged him tightly, and whispered in his ear, "That was the nicest, most surprising hello I have ever received. I loved it."

Harold laughed and said, "I meant it. You look spectacular."

She hugged him again. Little did he know that she had dreamed of this moment for a very long time.

Harold said, "Where are you taking me tonight Linda?"

"I know that you eat light, like salads, don't eat too much meat other than chicken or turkey, and drink lots of water. I know you like to work out, and the results are obvious. So, I thought we would go to a traditional Dominican Republic restaurant and you can order what you like."

"How do you know that about me Linda?"

"You are a very famous man. You are a baseball player, a business and farm owner, are intelligent, have a doctoral degree, love the outdoors, and like to travel on hunting and fishing trips to beautiful places in the world. I know that you are a Renaissance man Harold Gatewood."

"Thanks for the compliments."

"I am the president of your fan club and I have been doing research on you."

"You flatter me too much."

"I mean it Harold. I liked you from the first minute we met on the plane."

"I liked you also. I was hoping you would be sitting in the empty seat next to me when you were walking down the aisle."

"So was I."

"Well Linda, look how nice it has worked out."

She giggled and said that she agreed. She then suggested they head to the restaurant.

"Should I drive tonight Linda?"

"No. It is only a short distance. It will be nice to walk, plus we can talk on the way."

They held hands, talked, and laughed on the way to the Club de Cena Dominicana, the Dominicana Supper Club.

Harold asked, "What kind of food is on the menu?"

"Excepcionial y tradicional cocina Dominicana"

"Exceptional and traditional Dominican cuisine, correct?"

"Excellent Harold. You speak Spanish very well."

Gatewood laughed and said, "Linda, my high school Spanish teacher would disagree with you."

"Why?"

"Because after two years of it in high school she told me that she could write all the Spanish I knew on a postage stamp an she would have room left over."

"Oh stop it Harold. No one is that grammatically challenged after two years of classes. What did you tell her after she said that ridiculous comment to you?"

He laughed and said, "What could I say? It was true."

They entered and were ushered to their table. They talked for several minutes and were finally ready to order. Linda ordered guisados, which consisted of meat, fish, bell peppers, onion, garlic, celery, and olives, a house salad, and coffee with cream and sugar. Harold followed with moro de guandules, yellow rice with peas, olives and onions. He asked the waitress to substitute chicken for the traditional pork. He also had a house salad, and ice water to drink.

They talked and ate, being careful not to make a mistake of spilling their food or drinks. Linda recounted how one of her girlfriends would always try to make her laugh when they were eating. Harold told the story of one of his friends who had done the same thing. They both agreed that that was what friends were for. Harold asked about her childhood.

Linda said her parents had spilt up when she was young. The family was living in Nebraska at the time. After the divorce Linda moved to Brunswick, Maine where she stayed from age eleven through high school. She then went to college in California, and law school in Arizona, as she had mentioned on the plane.

Harold told her that he had spent all of his school years, kindergarten through high school, in Gibson City. He then went to his undergraduate and master's college years close to his home, and then started playing baseball. He earned a doctorate while he was still playing in the big leagues.

After dinner they danced to slow music at the restaurant, but avoided the fast ones, as Linda was wearing short heels and did not want to sprain her ankle. During the last slow dance Linda whispered in Harold's ear, "I have had fun tonight Harold."

"So have I Linda."

"Harold, I want you to take me back to the hotel now. I want to make love with you all night long."

Harold was surprised by her comment and looked into her eyes. She kissed him passionately, after which Linda honored her promise to take Harold to supper and paid the bill. Harold left the tip and they walked back to the hotel, talking and holding hands.

They rode the elevator up to the sixth floor, turned the key in the lock, shut the door, and kissed their way to the bed. Harold unzipped her dress in the back, and they both laughed as it made a "swoosh" sound as it slid down her body to the floor. They took turns helping each other out of their clothes, and were soon in bed.

They talked for a short time and then made love several times during the night, being interrupted by short naps in between the glorious events.

The next morning Linda was up early, getting ready for work. When it was time to leave she walked to the bed, sat down, and stroked Harold's hair. He responded and said, "Good morning."

She returned the comment, and then said that last night had been the nicest night of her life. Harold said that he had loved being with her and that she was even more wonderful that he had hoped. She said that she needed to go to work and that she would like to see him after supper tonight if he did not have other plans. He said that he did not have any plans and asked her what time was good for her.

"Nine tonight, after I finish work and clean up."

"Do you want to go out?"

"No, I want to stay in with you. Please come to my room."

"Okay. Do you need a ride to work?"

"No. My law firm is just down the street, at the intersection of Guillermo and Campos streets, Suite C."

"Okay. I will see you tonight."

Linda turned and started for the door. Harold sat up in bed and lovingly threw his pillow at Linda, softly hitting her in the back. Startled, she turned around, saw the pillow on the floor, started to laugh, and ran to the bed, jumped on Harold with the pillow in her hands and started to gently smack him with it. Soon both of them were laughing like school children.

She stopped and kissed him passionately, then said, "I love being with you Harold."

He returned the compliment, and then the kiss, and soon they were embraced in a passionate love-making session once again. After twenty minutes, she said that she had to go to work as she was late.

She kissed him gently and said, "We can pick this up again when I see you tonight." She then walked to the door. She stopped, turned around, smiled, and said, "I will see you at nine tonight Harold. Have a fun day." She then blew him a kiss and headed off to work.

He could not wait for her to return from work and be with him in the evening.

Their affection for each other grew during the time they were in the Dominican Republic. He remembered the first time he had told her that he loved her.

After rerunning from a hard day's work for the CIO, he had stopped at the gift shop in the hotel. He bought a bouquet of long-stemmed, bright-red roses, and rode the elevator upstairs to room one hundred. He opened the door, walked to Linda, handed her the roses, and said, "I love you."

Her eyes filled with tears and she said, "I love you too Harold. I have always loved you."

He thought that her second comment was unusual, but he was convinced that she meant what she had said. They kissed passionately, and moved to the bed, where they made love until the early morning hours.

As they continued to spend more and more time together, he became troubled, and wanted to find out more about her background.

He was very concerned about the inconsistencies that had been popping up in Linda's comments and actions. He needed to verify her background in order to prevent his doubts from negatively influencing their feelings for each other.

She had obviously lied to him about her office location and her employment. He needed to understand where she went each day when she said she was leaving for the office. Over the years he had faced danger many times, and had been crossed by people who he thought were friendly but had turned out to be disloyal. He cared for Linda but he needed validation that she was not involved in anything that could cause him trouble, as too many people were after his scalp.

Both he and Linda were up early and out the door, she to her "work" and he to meet a team owner in the league. After they kissed goodbye they walked in opposite directions. She strolled to the parking garage, stopping along the way at a drugstore to pick up some personal items. He quickly returned to the hotel and had the valet service bring his car around to the front of the building.

He drove to her parking garage and parked until she drove out. He stayed a safe distance behind her so he would not be seen, and followed her out of town to the barn that served as her storage facility. He parked behind a tree a few hundred yards behind the building and waited until she returned to her car and drove away.

When she was out of sight he drove to the barn, picked the lock on the door, and entered.

He was shocked at what he saw. A collection of computer equipment, firearms, bullet cartridges, a file drawer with financial records, makeup kits, false noses, contact lenses, wigs, fake moles and beauty marks, a file with the names and phone numbers of plastic surgeons, maps, a "weight suit" that could be worn under clothes to add weight to a person, and ten passports were stacked on and around a desk.

He read the passports, which were issued for American, British, French, Italian, and Spanish citizens, were all in different names, and listed with different weights and pictures. Georgia Reynolds, Tina Denver, Jacki Olson, Isidora Rozzilli, Livie Callis, Caro Rano, and Eva Bottcher were some of the false identities.

He sat down in the chair by the desk and said, "Who is Linda Westmorland? What does she want with me? Am I in danger from this woman who says she loves me?"

He sat and thought for a few moments and tried to think of who in the country knew he was here. His public contact had been limited to the hotel employees, people at restaurants, the domino players, the men at the barber shop, the vudu woman and her son Manuel, the baseball people he had talked with, the spectators at the games he had scouted, and Linda. He did not think that anyone he mentioned had a reason to cause him harm.

That left only the strangers who may have seen him at the ballpark, walking on the street, or those who may have read in the newspaper that he was scouting in the country. He had no clue who might be after his head, other than the usual cartel and AIO crowd. He decided to return to the hotel and call Rick Owens at the CIO.

"Hi Mam. This is Harold Gatewood for Rick Owens. Please tell him it is urgent."

"Just a moment Sir."

"Hi Harold."

"What do you have for me today?"

"Good news. I have a source who is helping me get information about the cartel deliveries into the country down here, and the shipments out of here to North America and Europe."

"Good work. Who is it?"

"It is a vudu woman and her son."

"How did you find them?"

"They lost two sons to the cartel. I was getting acclimated to the city and struck up a conversation with the old woman. Each day I worked out and then walked a route close to the hotel. Truthfully, the source just fell into my lap, as they sent me a note requesting contact."

"Is it a good source?"

"Yes. I went with the son last night to a cockfight and was able to identify and photograph several cartel workers. I am going to send the file to you when we are done talking."

"Great. We will identify them and follow up. We will want to observe their movements so do not try to apprehend them. We want them to be unaware that we are watching them. This is really good news Harold."

"That's not all of the good news Rick. I won around two hundred dollars on the cockfights."

Both men broke out in laughter.

"Do you have anything else?"

"Yes. Can you see if you have any information on a Linda Westmorland? She also may go by Georgia Reynolds, Tina Denver, Jacki Olson, Isidora Rozzilli, Livie Callis, Caro Rana, or Eva Bottcher."

"What is the situation?"

"She may be a freelance hit-woman."

"I will let you know."

"Thanks."

"Harold, be careful."

"I will."

His suspicions proved correct as she would later disappear from his life.

The desk clerk handed the note to Harold, and he read it. He then asked the desk clerk a question. "What time did Linda leave the note at the front desk?"

"She left it about seven-thirty this morning as she was heading to work."

Harold again started to walk toward the front door. He stopped in his tracks, and reread the message. He then sat down in a comfortable green chair and thought. Linda had left.

The note read, "Harold, I love you. We have grown so close over the last few weeks. You are the man with whom I want to spend the rest of my life. I want to have children with you and build a family. I have loved you since I first saw you. You were so kind and polite on the plane. You have always respected me. I have been ordered to go to Rome, Italy by my office to work with a client who has a problem. I do not know how long I will be required to be there. I will be in touch soon."

Harold looked out the window and tried to comprehend the note. He knew that she loved him. He also knew that she was fleeing for some reason. She did not work for a law firm and she did not have to go to Munich, Germany for work reasons. He wondered if she worked for the mob? He thought not but he was unsure.

He was also inclined to think that she did not work for the cartels. His reasoning was that she was on the run for a personal reason. Perhaps she was fleeing a man who was a past lover, and had threatened to kill her. If she had done something illegal she was running to prevent arrest.

He had no idea what the reason for her flight was, as he did not have the needed information to make a judgement. He did know that one thing was clear, she was gone.

After finishing his mission, he returned home and heard from her.

The trip home was a total blur. He remembered being picked up at the regional airport by his parents. They had then driven him to their house in Gibson City, where he stayed and slept for four days. He was a zombie, beaten physically and mentally to the point where he was unrecognizable. He was a shadow of his former self.

He did not speak of the attacks in the Dominican Republic. When he was healthy enough to return to his own home, he kissed his parents, drove home, and walked through the front door. He sat down in the chair by the window and looked for his friends, the birds and the squirrels. He was not disappointed as they were going about their usual daily activities. He watched them for an hour without saying a word.

He remained in the chair for two days as it seemed like the thing to do, and it offered him refuge. He left only to eat, shower, and clean up. His mind did not dwell on anything. Instead, he watched the birds and the squirrels.

His parents dropped by to check on him each day. He smiled, but only talked to them enough to convince them he was doing alright.

His cell phone rang on the seventh day he was back. He looked at the area code of the number of the calling party. He sensed it was important and answered.

"Harold, this is Susana. You also know me as Linda. We spent wonderful weeks together in the Dominican Republic. We are perfectly matched Harold. We are destined to be together. I know that you loved me as Linda. I can be whoever and whatever you want me to be. We can have a wonderful life together."

She continued, "You have figured out that I killed your lover, Juliana Callejas. She needed to go. She could have never made you as happy as I can, as Linda, or myself. You belong to me Harold Gatewood, and you are never going to get away. You are, and will be, mine forever."

Gatewood listened but did not speak.

Susana said, "I love you Harold. Please love me."

Harold did not answer, and hung up the phone. He knew what he must do.

Susana, then once again, disappeared from his life. He had continued his comeback to major league baseball in Tuscon, Arizona. He did well but was called into his manager's office near the end of the season for news about his career. He remembered the events clearly.

"Am I being sent all the way down below A ball?"

"No. You are going to play for Pat Sullivan in the major leagues. You got the call to return to the big leagues."

Harold jumped from his chair and yelled in glee. He and Scott Binder, his manager, then hugged each other and Harold told him how much he appreciated Scott's confidence in him in giving him his chance to get to back in the major leagues.

"You earned it Harold. Pat Sullivan wants you to be in Phoenix tomorrow for the evening game."

Harold was on cloud nine as he walked to his locker, dressed, wished his teammates well, and headed back to his apartment. He made all of the arrangements for paying his bills, packing, and making sure he left Hayward with the slate clean. He went to bed, but he could not sleep, as he was thinking about his return to where he belonged.

In the morning, he packed the car and headed North to Phoenix. The short drive went quickly. He went to the ballpark and took care of all the details related to his contract, and an apartment. He then ate lunch, checked into a motel, in his requested room of one hundred, for one night, as he would be in his apartment the next day. He relaxed for a while, and then headed back to the ballpark.

Pat Sullivan arrived at the stadium and welcomed Harold to the club. Harold told him how much he appreciated Pat's faith in him and promised to give his all for the team.

Sullivan replied, "I needed help right away Harold. I know you will do everything you can do to help us. By the way, I arranged for you to have uniform number ten, because that was your dad's number when he played on the All-American team that went to England and when he played in the minors."

"Thank you Pat. I appreciate that."

"I have you in the lineup, batting fifth. Have fun and enjoy yourself."

"I will Pat. We'll make things happen."

Harold then went to the locker room, met his teammates, and dressed for the game. He walked up the runway to the dugout, looked at the lineup card on the wall and saw his name in the fifth slot of the batting order as Pat Sullivan had said. He then limbered up, and took batting practice.

Harold then relaxed and took in all of the sights and smells he loved at the ballpark. The grass smelled clean, and the air smelled fresh, better than in the minor leagues. The stadium was beautiful. He looked at the bright blue-colored seats, the green-colored hitting background in centerfield, and the beautiful scoreboard. He was relishing every minute of his comeback.

The game began and Harold watched his teammates go down in order, three outs on weak ground balls to the infielders.

He then went to the area below the stands and stretched, hit ten balls off a hitting tee in the cage, and returned to the dugout.

When the bottom of the second arrived he donned his batting helmet, went to the on-deck circle, and took five practice swings at imaginary swings, reminding himself to keep his head down when he swung. The hitter before him led off the inning with a weak fly ball out to left field.

Harold walked from the on-deck circle and heard his named called, "The next batter is Harold Gatewood, number ten." The crowd of thirty-nine thousand one hundred fans gave him a nice round of applause, all mindful of his second successful comeback to the major leagues and the many tragic, dangerous, and inspirational actions that had marked the last few years of his life.

Harold tipped his hat and then riveted all of his thoughts on the pitcher, a left-hander with a hopping fastball. He stepped into the batter's box and intensely watched the pitcher's throwing arm. The pitcher would up and threw a four-seam fast ball. As it sped toward home plate, Harold watched the seams of the ball, kept his head down, took his stride into the pitch, and sent a screaming line-drive into right-center field for a single.

He rounded first base, smiled, and clenched his fist in glee. After he returned to first base, the first baseman patted him on the thigh with his glove and said, "Welcome back." The first base umpire called timeout and the ball was thrown to the Phoenix dugout as a remembrance of Harold's first hit in his return to the big leagues. The crowd had been watching to see if Harold was ready for his return, as many doubted he could play again due to his age.

With the hit, the crowd erupted and clapped for an extended time. Soon, they were on their feet in a standing ovation. Harold, with his fists clenched, raised both arms above his head and pounded the air in appreciation. Tears rolled down his cheeks as he thought of his dad. He was overcome with emotion.

As he stood looking at the cheering crowd, he suddenly felt a pain in his back, and fell to the ground. He laid in pain on the ground as blood rushed from his chest and back, soaking his uniform and the dirt near him. He labored to breath, and started to sink away. His life flashed before his eyes. He saw his dad, and his deceased wife Akemi, his one true love, and then his eyes closed. He was rushed to the hospital.

On a rooftop a far distance from the stadium a man in a ghillie suit stood up, broke down his sniper's rifle, removed his suit, and placed all of the items in a black-colored plastic bag. He removed his camo-colored face mask and also placed it in the bag.

The man, Ekain Koldo, smiled and said, "I have done what many others could not do. I have killed Harold Gatewood. I will surely be renamed the national commander of the AIO when I return to Madrid."

He then hurried down the stairs to the street and walked to the subway where he boarded his train and headed to his motel far away from the middle of the city. He entered his room and patted himself on the back for his accomplishment. He showered and decided that he should reward himself for his successful mission. He called an escort service and asked that a nice, beautiful young woman be dispatched to his room in an hour.

He listened to the news on television, as the shooting incident was being discussed non-stop. Precisely an hour later a knock was heard at his door. He looked through the door's peephole and smiled. He opened the door and smiled again. His order had arrived. She was a gorgeous black-haired young woman. She walked into the room, holding her hands behind her back.

Koldo said, "Welcome my dear. I am surprised and pleased that the escort service has sent a Native American for me." Koldo then walked toward the bed, with the young woman behind him. He said, "What is your name darling?"

The beautiful Native American girl said, "Susana." As she continued to walk toward Koldo she moved both hands from behind her back to a position in front of her. Her hand held a large, sharp knife. The steel blade of the knife glistened in the bright light of the motel room.

The woman said, "My name is Susana Richards. I have been following you and I know what you did."

As Koldo turned around to see his female guest, Susana thrust the large knife downward into Koldo's head, between the eyes.

Susana said, "And you will pay for killing the man I love, Harold Gatewood." She then proceeded to scalp Koldo in the same fashion she had used on the three men from the Palcer de los Lectores book publishing company.

Chapter 2

Surprise, Surprise

December 31

Gatewood awoke form his restless night's sleep and spent the day with Susana, trying to understand his dream. Their relationship had progressed from hate, to friendship, to passion, and now to love. She had progressed from jealous, out-of-control stalker to a world-class serial killer, then to a woman who loved him with all of her heart.

In Harold's mind she had progressed from a ruthless, possessed psychopath who had killed a woman he had loved, to an enemy, to a sexual playmate, to a woman of pleasant company, to a confidant, and to a woman he truly loved.

She had supported him, killed his enemies in Washington, D. C. and Paris, and had saved his life in Chile. He had helped her escape in Chile. They had enjoyed a strange, but binding meeting of their souls.

They had passed through all of the phases of true love, falling in love, becoming a couple, disillusionment, finding real lasting love, and entering the phase where they were a powerful force when they were together, joined as one. They had become one entity, and when they were together they needed no one else.

Today was New Year's Eve, and they would meet for supper with his friends from Gibson City, Elliott, and Foosland, then return home for conversation, and a night of love-making. At supper, he watched her as she socialized with his friends. She had always been a positive force who was there when he needed support. He remembered the end of his mission in the Ukraine when he had gone to Chicago to testify against Mayor Riccardo Gennaro.

After the shootout on the courthouse steps, Gatewood then entered, testified to the authenticity of the tape he had used to record Mayor Riccardo Gennaro's admission that he, Flurry, Kazimierz, Oakwood, and Paxton had all participated in numerous felonies related to the drug trade, prostitution rings, gun running, and political crimes that had become second nature in Chicago. Soon, they would all face trial, and imprisonment for their misdeeds.

Harold Gatewood walked from the courthouse, a hero once again. At the end of the first block, he saw the spectacularly beautiful Susana Richards leaning against her car. They both smiled at each other. She clapped her hands four times, and said, "I saw what you did on the courthouse steps, and in the courtroom. People say that what you did today makes it a certainty you will be the next governor of Illinois."

"That's what people are telling me. But, I would rather be your boyfriend, and make love to you day and night."

Susana walked to him, put her arms around his neck, kissed him passionately, and said, "You are not only my boyfriend, you are the only man I have ever loved, and will always love forever. And, I must really love you because I turned down twenty million dollars to kill you. As far as the making love arrangement, that is why I am here. We are going to Gibson City, and we are going to do that, day and night." She opened the car door, smiled, and said, "Get in my love."

Harold was happy when the evening was over and when he and Susana returned to his home. They made love, and then talked. Susana said, "Harold, I have something to tell you."

"What is it honey?"

"I am pregnant. You are going to be a father."

Harold was speechless.

She said that she had taken the home test after they had been together just before Halloween. She was two months along, and was feeling terrific. She had the "pregnancy glow" and was looking wonderful.

Harold asked how it could have happened. She laughed, and said, Harold, we make love all the time. You know about the birds and the bees."

He laughed and said, "Yes. But, I thought you told me that you could not conceive."

"The doctors have always told me that I couldn't. This is a miracle, a gift from heaven. I did not plan for this to happen. But, I have always loved you and always wanted to have your baby so we could be a family. Are you alright with this situation?"

He looked at her and said, "Yes, this is a wonderful. I love you. It is a shock Susana, but is a wonderful one."

They then talked about their plans for the future. She said, "Harold, I want to get out of the contract-killing business. I have enough money, the same as you do, for us to live the rest of our lives. We only have to figure out how we will do that, as our occupations are somewhat unusual. Once we know that, we can figure out where to live. I would like to live here, in Gibson City."

"Susana, I have wanted to get out of the spy business. I have one last mission to finish, and then I can walk away. I have had enough of the past, the nightmares, the PTSD, and the killing. I am happy that we will have a normal life."

They made love, and kissed each other good night. Susana fell asleep immediately, but he could not. He looked at her and said, "She has always been there to support me, and considering the fact that I do love her, this will work. We have gone through many things together Susana, and this one will be one of the most pleasant. I love you." He then wrapped his arms around her, closed his eyes, and went to sleep, dreaming of finally becoming a father.

The next two days passed quickly. When he took her to the airport they kissed at the gate, and he said, "Be careful honey, we have a baby on the way."

She replied, "No Harold we don't, we have two babies on the way."

He was dumbstruck with the news, and said, "I thought you said we are having one baby."

She laughed and replied, "No, I said I was pregnant, and that you were going to be a father."

He laughed, and said, "You know how to surprise me Susana."

She kissed him, and said, "We will love having two babies. I love you Harold."

He laughed and said, "That will be great honey. I love you too."

Chapter 3

"All we can get"

December 31

IN TOKYO, JAPAN, YUA HAYATO WAS CONDUCTING a meeting with her top assistant, Arta Ayumu, whose name meant "new dream". Ayumu had joined the Yakaza as a street gang member in his youth, and considered his life with the crime family as his "new dream", to be a respected Yakaza warrior.

He had been born in the country, fifty-five miles outside of the Tokyo city limits, to a family with seven sons, of which he was the last. He was now thirty years old, six-feet-four-inches tall, two hundred fifty-eight pounds in weight, with an Adonis-type build. He had dark black hair, and dark-brown eyes, a barrel chest, an acne-marked face, and an IQ that resided in the basement of the listings. He was dumb as an ox, and twice as strong.

While he was not totally devoid of creative thinking skills, he was invaluable as a dependable, wind up, loyal soldier who could be dispatched by Yua Hayato to deliver a message. He could effectively deliver an offer, or a brutally-painful beating or killing, either of which would get Yua's point across to the receiver of his wrath.

He had worked his way up the Yakaza structure, starting in the streets, and progressing to the inner circle over his fourteen years in the mafia family.

He had never married, and the Yakaza was his life. He had killed many times for the "family", and was a ruthless, barbaric warrior schooled in the art of torture and pain deliverance. He was feared by the Yakaza's rivals and appreciated by Yua Hayato for his blind loyalty.

Yua spoke to him, outlining his mission. "Arta, I have struck deals with Shamus Conri the leader of the Irish Order Of Workers For Freedom And Independence, the IOFFI, Conall Blair, the leader of the Scottish Patriots For Independence And Freedom, the SPFIF, and the Einion Cryfder, the leader of the Welsh Independent Sovereignty Alliance Movement, the WISAM, to furnish weaponry and ammunition for their new movements for independence from the British Empire."

"Arta, you will go to Chicago and deliver a message to Mayor Riccardo Gennaro. Tell him that I appreciated him agreeing to our request to buy additional pistols and ammunition. Tell him I will deposit his check in the offshore account once he delivers the goods to you, and arranges for clearance from the port authorities for the delivery of the pistols to Tokyo."

"How many will we be buying?"

"All we can get. The price is set so all you have to do is make sure Mayor Gennaro fulfills the order and helps you leave Chicago without any problems. You will stay on the ship and accompany it to Tokyo where we will take delivery of the order. We will pack the weapons inside the frozen tuna carcasses, as always do. We will have our man at the port authority expedite them through customs, without any problems."

"I understand."

"Don't let Gennaro change the details of the order. Be persuasive. If he tries, remind him that he has said that he always enjoys seeing the sun rise. Assure him that if he does not honor the deal I negotiated with him, that he will have seen his last sunrise."

Arta Ayumu agreed and left for the airport as he was booked on an evening flight to Chicago.

Yua Hayato sat back in her chair and sighed. Her work for the day was done. Her thoughts turned to her lover, Harold Gatewood. She had been sullen, and had missed him every day since their last visit time together. She wanted to be with him, have him hold her in his arms, and make love to her.

Her cousin Kimiko had been right, and he was also the best lover Yua had also enjoyed. She missed his presence, his touch, his tender lovemaking, and his successful "tattoo searches". She had never met anyone like him, and had fallen in love with him before she had even met him. She could not fathom being with any man other than him.

She remembered the first time she had seen him. He had been in Tokyo to talk with President Rida about the problems with North Korea in the China Sea.

For five days, Gatewood met with Rida and talked about cooperative strategy between their two countries. Each of those days he had thought about Yua Hayato. He had called her office and left a message on his fourth day in Tokyo, but she had not responded. He was disappointed, but he was too busy to worry about the rebuff by the beautiful crime family leader.

On Gatewood's last night last night in Tokyo he had walked to the ballpark, past the apartment building where he and Akemi had lived, and taken a seat behind home plate. He relaxed and watched the warmups on the field, but was slapped on the back by a Japanese man who was an employee of the Tokyo Cardinals.

Gatewood looked at the man and said, "Hiroshi Atsushi, how are you?" Hiroshi had been the team representative who had picked Gatewood up at the airport when he had signed with the Cardinals. After several minutes of conversation Gatewood said, "Hiroshi, I owe you a great debt of gratitude. You taught me how to respectfully bow to a Japanese lady, and that skill allowed me to meet my one true love in life, Akemi Gang, who became my wife."

After more conversation, said he had to leave. He returned shortly and told Gatewood he had made arrangements for Harold to throw out the first ball before the game started. It was a surprise and an honor.

Gatewood found himself standing on the pitcher's mound, ready to throw the ceremonial first pitch to home plate. The announcer said, first in Japanese, and then in English, "Cardinal fans, we have a treat tonight. The person throwing out the first pitch tonight is former Tokyo Cardinal star and major league veteran Harold Gatewood."

The crowd cheered and Gatewood threw a bullet to the catcher. He then raised both arms in the air, took off the Cardinals cap he had been given and saluted the thousands of fans.

In the sky box of the owners of the team, Yakaza crime boss Yua Hayato sat motionless, her eyes glued on Gatewood as he waved to the crowd, and as he smiled as he walked to the Cardinal dugout to shake hands with the players. She watched his every move until he was out of sight. She later found out where he was sitting and watched him with her binoculars throughout the game as he talked with fans and signed autographs. Her facial expression never changed, but her mind was running a million miles an hour.

She had not returned his call because she was afraid. She was fearful that if she were with him she would lose control, act like a young schoolgirl, and make a fool of herself.

Gatewood watched the entire game and then headed to a secret player's exit he had taken to escape thecrowds after he had showered, and was heading home after the game. He was in a hurry and had charged around a corner to get to the exit when he ran into a Japanese lady, knocking her off balance, but catching her before she fell to the floor.

He quickly said, "I am sorry. I apologize for running into you." After he had helped the woman regain her balance, he had his first chance to look at her. She was even more beautiful than he had visualized.

Gatewood still had a grip on the lady's arms, but neither seemed to mind. Even if they did they would not have been able to complain, as they just stood there looking into each other's eyes, and remaining silent. Gatewood then laughed and said, "Are you alright?"

The woman did not answer, but walked away. After walking ten feet, she stopped, turned again, and looked into Harold's eyes for a long period of time, then turned without saying a word, and walked away.

The next day, the twenty-eighth, Gatewood flew back to Beijing.

The beautiful Japanese woman sat in her office, thinking about her encounter with Gatewood. She dejectedly said, "I was so afraid I would not measure up to his standards when he had called me. When I bumped into him at the ballpark I could only look at him. I should have answered his calls, and then met him. I know we would have fun. I wanted to make love with him. Now I am afraid that I will never have another chance to do that."

Her missed opportunity had haunted her so much that she had flown to America and showed up unannounced on his doorstep. She remembered how nervous she had been when she had waited for him to answer the door.

Harold had been sitting in his favorite chair when he heard a loud knock on his front door. After opening the door he was shocked to see a beautiful woman standing in front of him on his porch. He was too stunned to talk.

She smiled seductively at him, and said, "Harold, I am Yua Hayato."

They looked into each other's eyes and smiled.

She smiled again and said, "I understand that you are interested in finding out the location of my tattoo."

She then walked to Gatewood, draped her arms around his neck, gently pulled him to her, and kissed him passionately. She then looked into his eyes and said, "Well Harold, are you just going to stand there, or are you going to start your search?"

The results of her visit had been so successful that she had known that they were destined to be together. They had enjoyed themselves so much that she had returned a second time to Gibson City, Illinois to be with him.

I had waited in her rental car while he had spoken with the conservative politicians of Illinois who wanted him to run for governor of the state. After a few more minutes of discussing the situation, the three political leaders left, and Gatewood sat down in his family-room chair and watched his friends the birds and the squirrels.

Five minutes later another knock on the front door was heard. Harold got up from his chair, and headed toward the door, thinking, "I wonder what those guys forgot to take with them."

He opened the door, and then stood silently, with a surprised look on his face. I had done my best to look beautiful, and I was standing on his porch smiling at him. I said, "I was in Chicago on business, and wanted to surprise you. I have missed you."

I then moved to him, draped my arms around his neck, and kissed him passionately. He then took my left hand in his right, and walked with me to the bedroom where we made love for over an hour.

When they were done, I gently stroked his face with my left hand and said, "Harold, I love you. And, I don't believe in the Gatewood Sweetheart Curse. I will always be in your life."

Gatewood looked at me, kissed her passionately, and said, "That's what they all say. We'll see what happens."

I knew he had been hurt many times, and had lost several women who had been his lover. I wanted to be with him, love him, and make sure he would never be hurt again. I invited him to come with me to the Isle of Shima when he had free time.

He arrived in Tokyo, and filed from the plane to the gate area, ever-mindful of who might be waiting for him in the terminal, a habit that had saved his life when he had returned to Chicago from Paris and had been attacked by the USFF in the past.

Luckily, the only waiting person to greet him was me. He walked to me, smiled, kissed her, and said, "This is the best welcoming committee I could have ever hoped for." We then walked hand-in-hand to the parking garage where we hopped in my car, a beautiful dark-black-colored Mercedes, and left the terminal.

Once on a deserted side-street, I laughed and jammed the accelerator to the floor, causing Harold's head to bob like a cork on the water. We both laughed, and he remembered a similar experience with my now- deceased cousin and former Yakaza family head Kimiko Hayato.

The incident had taken place after he had played his first game for the Tokyo Cardinals and was walking back to his apartment.

After my cousin had pulled her flashy, red BMW to the curb, and asked if he wanted a ride, Harold had walked around the car to the passenger side, slid into the bucket seat, looked at his beautiful new chauffer Kimiko, and smiled.

She had smiled back, then shifted the car into drive, pushed the accelerator down hard, and sped forward, causing Harold's head to jerk back, and his voice break out into a loud, hilarious laugh. His response was met by hers, a relaxed, giggly, soft, seductive type of laugh which helped form an instant bond between them.

The laughing had continued for four blocks, until the car pulled up to the curb in front of Harold's apartment building. They were laughing like school children who knew they were about to get away with something that the teacher would not be able to stop.

Harold had then said, "That was fun. When did you get your pilot's license?"

"A few years ago."

"What altitude were we at the last four blocks?"

"We were still on the ground, but we can try it again to see if we can gain altitude this time, if you like."

"As much as I would like that, I would hate to show up at the ballpark tomorrow with a stiff neck."

"We wouldn't want that."

Now, he had had flight number two with the second beautiful Yakaza crime princess, me. We laughed, and I said, "I am a much better low-flying pilot that Kimiko."

"You are much better at everything that Kimiko."

I then squeezed his hand and. "I have developed a new, special treat for you in the love-making department that we are going to try as soon as we get to my apartment."

"Then by all means Yua, speed up again."

I again floored the accelerator, our heads flew back again, and we laughed as I sped toward the apartment. Once inside we kissed their way to the bedroom and made love repeatedly until we were exhausted.

We then talked about their plans for his stay. We would spend a week in Tokyo, then head to the Isle of Shima for a week, then return to Tokyo until he had to leave.

We relaxed, worked out, visited the shrines and temples Tokyo, walked in the nearby park, spilt our time eating in restaurants and at my apartment, watched three baseball games from the sky box that my Yakaza family still owned and used to entertain the high-roller gamblers who visited Tokyo, and made love each night.

The second week we drove South from Tokyo along the coastline, admiring the ocean, talking, and stopping two times for walks along the beach. The soft sand was comforting to our bare feet after we had removed our shoes, and the sound of the waves hitting the shore soothed our minds.

We listened to the sea gulls as they walked, which caused him to say that the bird's sounds were some his favorite things about walking on the beach. We made slow progress as they often stopped, put our arms around each other and kissed.

The coastline drive was pretty, and we followed it to Isle of Shima. The location was seventy-five miles South of Nagoya and on the opposite side of the peninsula from Osaka. We looked at the coastline dotted with pine trees, admired the soft sandy inlet, the pebble-strewn bays, and the emerald and indigo-colored waters of Toba Bay, located on the Northeastern end of the Isle of Shima.

We checked into their our room, showered, then took a nice walk, and watched a beautiful sunset as evening arrived. We then ate dinner, made love, and slept soundly until morning, draped in each other's arms.

The Isle of Shima was famous for its cultured pearls, and the women divers who free-dived, holding their breath for a minute or more as they swam to the floor of the sea to harvest sea urchins, sea weed, agar-agar, spiny lobsters, abalone, and oysters that had produced cultured pearls.

We watched the women divers, the ama-san, exit from their huts, called amgoyas, say a prayer to the sun goddess Amatesrsasu for safety from sea monsters and a safe return home. They would also pray to the goddess of the sea, Ishigami, would grant each diver one wish in their lifetime.

The traditional costume of a white-cotton garment had been replaced by a white-colored dive suit rumored to repel sharks and jellyfish, and an ornate red symbol worn on their forehead shaped like star, called a seiman, or a doman, a pentagram-shaped figure, both believed to fight the evil that might befall the divers. A pair of gloves, goggles, and a knife, completed the diver's uniform.

The women diver's job was to harvest oysters from the sea in hopes of finding cultured pearls that would be used to form the world's most beautiful necklaces, earrings, and other pieces of jewelry. They would also return the oysters to the sea floor after inserting a foreign object in them, so that a pearl could be formed. The divers would also move the oyster beds if danger was expected from a red tide condition, or from a typhoon.

The life of a diver was hard, as they originally dove twice a day for up to thirty minutes each dive. They would dive to the sea floor, weighted down with a string of weights tied around their waist, and tethered to a wooden basket floating on top of the water by a rope. They would harvest their catch, and then surface, letting out a whistling sound, called an isobue, and then catching their breath.

Harold and I watched them dive, then warm up by fires build on the shore near their huts to recover from their dives into the deep, cold water.

The old, traditional ways were dying, and were being replaced by the mechanized cultured pearl farming where an irritant would be placed inside the oyster shell, and the oysters were kept in areas inside a building.

The process was faster and more efficient. It yielded many pearls, most of which were too dark in colored, not round, were cloudy in appearance, or had other flaws, making them unacceptable for the best jewelry use. But, the pearls that made the grade were still magnificent, and adorned the beautiful, deeply-desired jewelry owned by the world's most affluent people.

The process to develop a cultured pearl took three years. Once an irritant was placed inside the soft tissue of the oyster, a secretion, called a nacre, was naturally issued by the oyster to fight the invasion of the irritant. Layer after layer of nacre was then issued, forming over the irritant until a pearl was formed, then harvested.

We also visited the beautiful shires in the area, walked the beach, admired the sunsets, relaxed, made love, and enjoyed each other's company. The ama-sans were not the only people diving during the week, as Harold regularly tattoo-dived for my tattoo, which led to pleasure for both of us.

The week went by much too fast, and we returned to Tokyo. When we went to bed in my apartment, after making love, I said, "Harold, I love you very much. I had such a wonderful time with you, like we always do. I want you to live with me here in Tokyo. I can arrange to have you made the manager of the Tokyo Cardinals. You can leave the spy business, return to baseball, and we can be together."

He said, "I love you too Yua. We are good for each other. Let me think about that, alright? I love being with you, and I have always liked living in the Orient."

"It was the best two weeks of my life, and I want it to continue until I pass from this earth. I have decided that we will be together. Of I can't be with him, then no other will be either. I have killed before, and I will do so again to prevent Harold from being with any woman other than me."

Chapter 4

"It is nice to meet you."

December 31

IRINEI ARTYOM's PLNE LANDED ON TIME AT the Chicago airport. After retrieving his suitcase, he picked up his rental car, and headed to his hotel located near the famous "Miracle Mile" shopping area. He checked in and then took a taxi to Mayor Riccardo Gennaro's office.

He spoke to the mayor's secretary, giving her his name and his appointment time, and then took a seat in the waiting room while he waited for the mayor. As he waited, he thought about how Bogdan Vsevlod had ended his tenure as the head of the SBP mafia. He recalled every detail.

In Moscow, Russia, Ininei Artyom, Kilmet Vaska, and Ilia Borya sat in Vaska's office at the end of the day and discussed what action they should take. The Solntsevskeya Bratva Pravda was a mess. It was hemorrhaging money in its Chicago operation, and Bogdan Vesvlod was AWOL from his role as Pakhan of the organization.

Artyom had always coveted the role of leader of the mafia, and had been plotting his takeover from Vsevlod for many years. He sensed that the time for action was now. Vaska and Borya agreed, and the three upper management members set a plan for a change in management for the SBP.

Vesvlod was in a deep state of depression due to Karina Prekrasnyy's death. He remembered the last time he had spoken to her. He had called her at Kilmet Vaska's office. He was greeted by her sweet voice. He had asked, "Karina, how are this morning my love?"

"I am fine Bogdan. Thank you for asking."

"I was worried about you, as I called you last night and there was no answer."

"I was not feeling well and went to bed early to sleep. I am better now."

"Good. I was wondering if you would like to go to dinner with me tonight. We can go to your favorite restaurant, the one that has kulebiaka, the fish pie with eggs, rice, onion, and dill. You always love that place. It has the dance show where they do the hopak, the Ukrainian national dance where they do the squad and kick moves, the prisyadka."

"Do you mean the Cossack dance?"

"Yes. We have not been out much lately and I want to make it up to you Karina. I am sorry for the way things have been lately but I have been worried about the operations in Moscow and Chicago."

"Bogdan, let's do it another time. I still am not feeling well.'

The sting of her rebuke, and her flee from Russia to escape him, had crushed his spirits. Personally, he realized he had become a total failure, as he had lost his life's love, Karina Prekrasnyy, to a washed-up ex-baseball player and American CIO agent named Harold Gatewood, the man who had recently caused he and his prostitution rings in Moscow and Chicago trouble.

He was mixed up emotionally, as he wanted to kill Gatewood in the most gruesome and painful manner imaginable. He also was broken-hearted, and wanted to do whatever it took win back Karina, if it was not too late.

He had been shocked that Karina had been killed, and blamed Chicago Mayor Gennaro for her death. He was positive that she would have not testified against him in America. He also felt that she would have claimed that she falsified the information that had tied him to Gennaro's corrupt administration.

He was losing his grip on reality, and his life was spiraling downward. He had not done his job as pakhan for the SBP since she had left Moscow. The mob's prostitution business in Chicago was teetering on the edge of disappearance, and he was responsible. Try as he might, he could not function anymore.

He walked to his office the next morning, and had decided to ask Irinei Artyom to take over until he returned to good health. He walked into his office with his request on his lips. The words would never leave his mouth until it was too late.

A vicious blow to Vsevlod's head sent him crashing to the floor, where he was immediately pounced upon by Artyom, Vaska, and Borya. He was bound with rope, his hands behind his back, and his ankles tied together. He was blindfolded and a handkerchief was stuffed in his mount to prevent him from talking.

The three attackers then told him that he was being ousted from his leadership role due to his failure to take care of business, and for the near-collapse of the prostitution business in Chicago. He tried to speak but the handkerchief in his mouth prevented it.

Artyom spoke, "You are done. You can never return to run the SBP. We are going to silence you. You will be killed and buried as a disgrace to our mafia family. I know that you would probably like to say that you will volunteer to give up the reigns of the organization, leave Moscow, and never associate yourself with us again. We would never believe that, as we know you would soon be back trying to regain your position."

Vsevlod struggled to speak again, but no audible sounds escaped his throat.He was then taken down the back stairway to an awaiting car, and thrown in the trunk. He was then taken to a deserted, wooded area thirty miles outside the Moscow city limits.

When the car was stopped, he was taken from the trunk and thrown on the ground. Borya started to dig a deep grave. Vsevlod struggled to speak, but was unable to communicate. Borya continued to dig until the grave was six feet deep. He then threw his shovel on the ground and looked at Artyom.

Artyom signaled for his two co-harts to pick up Vsevlod and throw him in the grave. After Bogdan's body crashed to the ground inside the grave, Borya picked up his shovel and started throwing dirt into the grave. When the dirt stared to cover Vsevlod's chest, he screamed into the handkerchief in his mouth in a plea for his life.

When the shovelful of dirt covered his mouth he was silenced forever. Borya filled up the grave, placed his shovel in the trunk, and the three men headed to the SBP office in Moscow to start a new chapter for the SBO mafia.

On the drive to the office, Irinei Artyom was joyous. He had risen to the pinnacle of his career path, the Pakhan of the SBP. He had reached the top of the mountain. He knew he must be diligent and productive in his position, or someday he might be buried alive.

Artyom was a man of violence, but even he had been haunted by Bogdan Vesvlod's screams of fear and death. Artyom had buried men live before, but none of them had been a close friend like Vesvlod. As he continued to think about the gruesome murder, his thoughts were interrupted by the voice of Mayor Riccardo Gennaro. "Welcome Irinei Artyom, please come in to my office."

After exchanging small talk, Artyom spoke, "I appreciate you seeing me Riccardo. I know it is New Year's Eve, and I am sure you have several parties and functions to attend tonight.I wanted to tell you that it is nice to meet you. We have known each other, but Bogdan was running the SBP and handled personal discussions with you."

"It is nice to meet you in person also Irinei. We have done business with the SBP for many years, and it has always been a pleasant, and profitable, association. We hope to continue to do business with you. How is Bogdan?"

Irinei was able to keep a straight face, and answered, "That is why I am here. Bogdan has not been feeling well, and has gone underground where no one will find him. I am taking over his duties."

"I hope he feels better soon."

"We all hope he will. Both of you had agreed to a new arrangement in our business partnership in the prostitution business here in Chicago. we hope to continue that agreement with you."

Gennaro sensed an opportunity increase his take from the operation, and said, "That agreement was with Bogdan, and he is no longer with the SBP, if I am understanding you correctly. We have relied on his experience and expertise to run the SBP operation here. If he is out of the picture we are afraid that you might not have the experience to ensure the success will continue. I am not belittling your ability, but you may need time to gain the experience level that Bogdan possessed. If that is the case, we may need to increase our fee for allowing you to operate in Chicago."

"I understand your concern, but the SBP, myself included, has worked effectively with you before. We still have the same policies and procedures in place to keep the operation on an even keel. And, as you yourself has said, our stable of ladies is the best in the business."

"Yes, you are right about that. The quality of your ladies is the best in the city. But, we are concerned about profits. And, our expenses are always increasing."

"Riccardo, we want to increase our business operation in Chicago, but we want to operate under the agreement Bogdan and you negotiated in good faith. If our expenses increase we may be forced to place those funds in our other operations, perhaps in the Philippines, or Viet Nam."

"I understand Irinei. We value your business. Let's do this, we will leave the agreement I negotiated with Bogdan in place for one more year. Then, we will take a look at it to see if it is still viable. Do you agree?"

"That sounds fair. I do have one other concern Riccardo. We both have one other thing in common, the Harold Gatewood situation. He tends to leave dead men littered around the world. He has killed our operative Eveny Khariton in Poland. And, I know he killed your security head Nino Renzo here in Chicago."

"Yes Irinei, he did. I remember Eveny Khariton. He killed Adela Igone, her mother, and her cousin. And, we did lose a good man in Nino Renzo."

"Yes, I remember Nino. He killed Karina Prekrasnyy for us in Washington, D. C. We appreciated your help in that situation Riccardo."

"Irinei, what do you suggest be done with Harold Gatewood?"

"I think that an unfortunate, untraceable accident befall Mr. Gatewood."

"I agree. Let's work together to make that happen."

Chapter 5

The World Goes On

January 5

AN OVERNIGHT WINTER STORM HAD HIT CENTRAL Illinois, and the snowfall total had reached fourteen inches, covering everything in sight with mounds and mounds of beautiful, white snowflakes. It was rumored that each snowflake had its own unique shape, never to be duplicated again. While Gatewood could not prove the statement himself, he took it at face value.

The statement also reminded him of Susana Richards, his now-pregnant lover, as she was unique in appearance, temperament, and occupation. She had looked very beautiful during her visit, as her "pregnancy glow" was in full bloom. She was giddy with excitement about having two babies.

He was still in shock, as neither of them had planned on ever hearing the surprising news. As he looked out the window at the piles of snow that filled the yard, and blocked his lane from the road to his house, he realized that he was snowed in, probably for days.

He had an ample supply of food, as he always prepared for a Winter day such as today. He was prepared for a snowstorm, but he was still unprepared for fatherhood. He was happy, but overwhelmed. He laughed when he thought about what laid ahead for Susana and he. He knew she would be a good mother, and a dedicated, loving wife.

He also knew he would be a good father, once he became used to the idea. He had looked forward to having a family when he was married to Akemi, and she was pregnant with Tai. Unfortunately, that dream ended when they were killed by Masaru Hayato, Kimiko Hayato's brother, and Yua Hayato's cousin.

Harold knew that the news about the two babies would change Susana's and his lives dramatically. She would give up her unusual occupation, and he would give up his government work. Maybe he would become a major league manager.

He knew that managing the Tokyo Cardinals was now out the window, as having two dangerous women, his wife and Yua Hayato, together would end up in tragedy. He might join Pat Sullivan as a coach, or have his agent, Randle

Quinn, find him a manager's job. It would be a monumental change, but one he was willing to make because he did love Susana.

He walked to the pool table and worked on his game for forty-five minutes, to no avail. His mind remained on his fatherhood, and how his life would be altered. He poured himself a glass of water and returned to the window to look at the Winter wonderland in front of him.

He turned on the television to listen to the news about the world's events. He watched, and took note of the events that had taken place in the last few days after Susana had left. In Sweden, another rape had taken place. A young woman, Catrine Marti, twenty-three years of age, had been gang-raped by five men, all illegal immigrants from Syria, Afghanistan, and Northern Africa.

Sweden was Scandinavian country located in Northern Europe. Norway bordered the country on the North and West, Finland did likewise on the East, and the Baltic Sea caressed its border on the West. A bridge and a tunnel to Denmark connected the beautiful country of Sweden to the mainland of Europe.

The country was productive, had a highly-rated lifestyle characterized by high income per capita, clean air, beautiful scenery, and a total of ten million educated, healthy, wonderful people. Unfortunately, the politics of the country was rooted in liberalism.

The head of the country was a monarch, a king, and the actual grinding of the governmental gears was accomplished by a Prime Minister, and houses of elected leaders. The country had remained neutral during both World War I and II, and had successfully straddled the fence on political issues.

Outdoor activities were numerous, with fishing, hiking, camping, sailing, skiing, curling, and snowboarding among the choices. In fact, Gatewood had once planned on fishing for Northern Pike in the Baltic Sea off the coast of Stockholm, but had cancelled his trip due to a call to duty from the CIO.

The Southern part of the beautiful country was home to agriculture, and the Northern area was home to forests and logging. Coastal islands and inland lakes also dotted the landscape of the beautiful country. The climate was mild, with four identifiable seasons. The population was made of Germanic, native Swedish, and Viking-related peoples.

Sweden's crime rate was low, and the country was safe, and unlike Chicago, Illinois' "shooting gallery", was virtually free of gun violence. Security was handled by a national police force, and a SWAT division to handle terror situations.

Recently, due to the increasing violence and the resulting decreasing quality of life caused by the illegal immigrants Sweden had agreed to allow into the country, a Special immigration Task Force had been organized to address the immigrant problem.

The decision to accept the illegals had turned into a disaster, one which the country had rebelled against. The resulting governmental action was to admit their mistake, and to declare that no more illegal immigrants would be allowed to enter the country.

As in almost all countries that had accepted the illegals, the new arrivals did not accept their new country, its traditions, customs, and laws. The illegals had no intention to assimilate into their new country's culture and way of life. Instead, they behaved like animals, refusing to work, learn the language, and causing the crime rate to rise through theft, robbery, beatings, rapes, and murders.

In particular, rape of the country's women had become a major problem. The actual statistics reflecting the increase in crime caused by the illegals arrival had been kept secret by the government. The reason for the secrecy was unknown, but perhaps it was kept hidden due to fear, shame, or a refusal of the government to admit that the country's policy of accepting the illegals had been a total failure.

Catrine Marti was a beautiful blond-haired, blue-eyed, statuesque young woman of five-feet-seven-inches in height, and one-hundred-fifteen pounds in weight. She had inherited the best of the gene pools of her father, a photography and camera shop owner, and her mother, a homemaker.

She was intelligent, with a degree in fine arts from the well-respected Stockholm University, was quick witted, and wrote poetry in her spare time. Her work had been published in several journals, and she was dedicated to her craft.

She worked for her father in the store, and wrote after work. She hoped to become a fulltime writer, and according to many people in the know, had the drive and talent to make her dream materialize.

She was the older of two children in the family, was athletic, serving as a cheerleader and a member of the ski team in high school. She had many friends, female and male, and was an outgoing, charming lady who was usually the center of attraction in her peer group. She was an organizer, and had served as the ramrod to book trips and events with her friends.

She had organized a seven day holiday for seven of her friends to join her in the upcoming July to the island of Visby, in the Baltic Sea.

Cobblestone streets, quaint Swedish-style homes, beautiful beaches, a medieval- walled city, museums filled with native Swedish culture and artifacts, a world-class art museum, a nature preserve, a science center, a cave tour that featured stalactites and fossils, city parks, windmills, and lighthouses all were available for their enjoyment.

Catrine had finished her day's work at the photography and camera store, and had left to meet her friends a coffee shop to discuss the costs of the July trip, and then make reservations. She was excited, and proud of herself for the work she had done to put the trip together for she and her friends.

She decided to take a shortcut trough a park that would save her five minutes walking time, as she was already late. Shen she entered the park she saw five Syrian and North African men standing by a bench to her left. She quickly moved past them, as she had heard the warnings from her parents about the troubles the illegals were causing in town.

She heard footsteps behind her and increased her pace, hoping to leave the park, turn right and walk the half-block to the coffee shop where her friends were waiting for her. She felt a blow to her head, and fell to the ground. Immediately, the five illegal immigrant men pounced on her, pawing at her breasts and crotch, and ripping her clothes off.

They took turns raping her, over and over. She had screamed for help until the men had placed their hands over her mouth, then stuffed a dirty handkerchief into it. She was helpless, and suffered the indignities for what seemed like an eternity.

When they had finished the five illegals laughed, kicked her while she was prone on the ground, and then left. They believed they had the duty and right to rape Catrine, as she was an infidel, and a non-believer in Islam. She was found by a passerby, who called the police for help.

Catrine Marti was then taken to the hospital. She was suffering from shock, given a rape kit test, and diagnosed as a victim of the crime that was rapidly escalating in Sweden, rape. She was stabilized and remained in the hospital overnight.

The incident had taken place in a small coastal town South of Stockholm, the capital of the country. The family had lived in a charming, laid-back, small town of two thousand population for four generations. Recently, against the wishes of the citizenry, the national government had forced the town to take, house, and accept four hundred illegal immigrants from Syria and North Africa.

The results had been detrimental to the townspeople, as the typical problems related to the illegals' crime activities and their refusal to blend into the Swedish way of life had come to haunt the beautiful little burg. The tension between the townspeople and the illegals had deteriorated to a point where violence might erupt.

News of the rape spread quickly in the town, and a mob was formed to search for the five illegal immigrant assailants. They were found in the same park, as they had returned after the incident. Words were exchanged, and soon violence erupted. The vigilantes made the illegals pay their dues for raping Catrine, beating the illegals to near death.

Police were called when the fight broke out but the police, having reached their breaking point from dealing with the illegals, took their time to arrive at the scene, arriving after the vigilantes has dispersed.

All five of the illegals had severe injuries which ranged from contusions, lacerations, and broken bones to concussions. The rape and follow-up incident were now the talk of the country, and had highlighted the Swedish government's failed policy to accept the illegal immigrants into the country.

Gatewood closed his eyes and thought, "None of it should have never happened. When will the world learn that the acceptance of illegal immigrants who will not assimilate into the country will never work."

Chapter 6

Afghanistan

January 5

"BAILEY AND SMITHERS, YOU ARE ON RECON DUTY today. Take you Humvee and scot the area towards town and make sure no IED'S are planted along the road."
"Yes Sir."
First Lieutenant Jeff Bailey was on his third tour of Afghanistan, and Private First Class Aaron Smithers was on week shy of completing his first tour.
Smithers as a high school graduate from Enid, Oklahoma who had enlisted after graduation. He was single, five-feet-four-inches tall, and weighed one-hundred-forty pounds. He had taken a lot of abuse from his drill instructor in basic training about being a "runt" but he was tough and had graduated from boot camp and advanced infantry training, then had volunteered for a tour in Afghanistan.
He was no Rhodes Scholar, and had joined the army because his options were limited. His grandfather and father had been career army men, and he wanted to follow their paths. He was Bailey's driver, and due to his history of racing stock cars while he was in high school, he performed his duty flawlessly.
Jeff Bailey was the opposite of Aaron Smithers. He had graduated from Boston Technical University with a degree in advanced technological sciences, had served in the ROTC program, and had entered the army after graduation. He volunteered for duty in Afghanistan, and had re-upped two more times.
He was married, with two little girls, aged four and three, and a beautiful wife, at home in Frisco, Missouri. He was a true believer, and wanted to contribute to America's mission in Afghanistan. He loved his work, and planned on re-upping again when his tour of duty ended in September.
He and Smithers were the odd couple, but operated efficiently in the field. Today's mission faced the usual dangers of being in the field, and were always subject to unseen events.

As they chugged down the road, their Humvee, a four-wheel-drive military light truck named the high Mobility Multipurpose Wheeled Vehicle, was the vehicle of choice in Afghanistan, and was used to replace the "jeep", serve as an ambulance, and a commercial utility cargo vehicle. In the Gulf War, it was proficient in handling the desert terrain, and performed admirably.

The Humvee had replaced the its predecessors in reconnaissance missions and was outfitted with four doors, over-sized tires, an open or closed roof that could house firepower, a large, powerful engine, four seats, bullet-proof glass windows, high ground clearance, and a strong chassis.

Early losses of personnel were caused by a lack of armor plating. One thousand pound armor plates were bolted to the floor and on the sides near the wheel wells to solve the problem of blasts from underneath the vehicle that could kill or injure the occupants.

Additional improvements included an automatically controlled sighting and firing of the weaponry that was included in the vehicle. An operator could fire from within the Humvee, safe from enemy fire. Weaponry could include light and heavy machine guns, grenade launchers, and surface-to-air missiles.

Latches had also been added to the outside of the doors to allow the doors to be jerked off by another vehicle if the four soldiers would be trapped inside the Humvee. The vehicle was not totally safe from enemy fire, but the improvements had increased the safety of the troops when inside.

Bailey and Smithers were brave soldiers, but still operated on a "safety first" approach to their duty. They were comfortable in the Humvee. Attacks against their type of vehicle were usually carried out by the use of IED'S, improvised explosive devices, that were set off by actions other than what took place in regular military actions.

Guerrilla warfare tactics were used to arm and initiate a device such as an artillery round with a detonator that would cause the round to explode. Roadside bombs were the order of the day in Afghanistan. Syria, and Iraq.

Assassination attempts, and the blowing up of buses, cars, tanks, and military vehicles were common uses of IED's. Suicide bombers armed with IED's also created problems in the war theater and in the civilian world. The device could be as simply designed as using a switch to activate the charge, an initiator such a fuse, a container such as an artillery round, a charge, also called the explosive material, and a power source such as a battery to remotely set off the explosion.

Infrared devices, remote controlled detonators, magnetic triggers, pressure-sensitive triggering devices, or trip wires could also be used with the IED's. In Afghanistan, the "bombs' could be placed in animal carcasses, pop cans, boxes, or high on a pole or tree to kill, or injure a target by causing loss of limbs.

IED's had been used by terrorists for many years. Chechen rebels, with whom Gatewood was familiar, had used pressure cooker bombs to blow up crowds of civilians. The IOFFI in Ireland, had used remote controlled, radio controlled, infrared light beam activated, mercury-tilt switch activated IED's to blow up cars, politicians, and enemies since the late nineteen-sixties.

The devices would work anywhere, in culverts, ditches, and even in the open, and cause death and destruction.

Smithers' main interest, other than car racing, was hunting. As he and Bailey approached an intersection they talked about turkey hunting. Smithers' goal was to earn the Grand Slam of turkey hunting by shooting an Eastern, a Merriman, a Rio Grande, and an Osceola species. He had a Merriman to his credit. Although Bailey had never gone turkey hunting, he was interested in Smithers' knowledge and passion about the sport.

Smithers continued to speak, and glanced to his right and left as he approached the intersection. "The hardest turkey species to shoot is the Osceola, which lives in Florida. It takes a great deal of patience to get one as they are rare, and very skittish. They often approach the decoy, and then…"

Before Smithers could finish his sentence, a loud boom was heard. Smithers lost control of the Humvee, and it jerked violently, then fishtailed from right to left, then headed toward a high utility pole on the left side of the road. Bailey was tossed to the right, then the left, in his seat. His seatbelt snapped due to the stress of the vehicle's violent movements, and he was free-floating in his seat.

Smithers' seat belt had not failed, and he was struggling to regain control of the Humvee. The vehicle was heading straight toward the utility pole at a speed of fifty miles an hour. Smithers' looked up and saw that the pole was directly in front of him. He jerked the steering wheel to his left to avoid crashing into the pole and sending it directly into his body.

Bailey, still free-floating in the cab due to his seat belt's failure, pushed his right hand and arm ahead against the front dashboard to try to brace himself for the rapidly approaching impact. He and Smithers looked at each other for an instant. Both had fear in their eyes. They turned their attention back to the pole in front of them. Smack! The Humvee crashed into the pole, sending both men forward.

Smithers' body surged forward, then was violently snapped backwards when his seat belt prevented any further forward movement. His neck also jerked back violently when the Humvee.

Bailey had flown forward into the windshield, his legs crashing against the dashboard of the vehicle. He heard a loud snap, and then he lost consciousness.

Both men laid in the vehicle, unaware of their surroundings, and unprepared if an enemy attack on the ground would follow the IED explosion. After an hour, when they had not reported in to headquarters with their location, a second Humvee appeared, placed them in the vehicle and sped toward the base hospital, where they were admitted and their injuries were treated.

Both men were badly injured, and would never return to active duty. Smithers' neck vertebrae were severely injured. Luckily, his spinal cord had not been shattered. He underwent months of therapy and psychiatric treatment for his role in the incident. He was never the same after the attack, and was released from the army thirteen months after the wreck, disabled and unable to work due to the constant pain and headaches he battled until his death at age thirty-one.

Bailey suffered two broken legs, a broken wrist from bracing himself against to dashboard, over one hundred stiches in his face that left permanent scars under his left eye and on his right cheek. He battled depression and nightmares related to his inability to shake the memories of his body flying toward the windshield.

He was despondent by his discharge from the army, and the failure of his legs to properly heal, which caused him to walk with a cane the rest of his life. His mobility was severely limited, and he was on pain medication for the rest of his life. He was a proud soldier who was forced to leave the military due to the attack.

He remained a proud father and husband, raised his two daughters, both of whom entered the armed forces, and worked for the Veteran's Administration as an advocate for injured soldiers returning to civilian life after being injured in war-related incidents. He died at age fifty-nine.

Both men were casualties of a terror-related incident. As Gatewood heard the news reporter move on to the next story he thought, "Dam terrorists. They have to be stopped."

Chapter 7

Columbia, South Carolina

January 5

FIFTEEN-YEAR-OLD LIBBY CURTIS CALLED HER BFF, "Best Female Friend", Harper Kingdon, and urged her to join her on a trip to the Apex Mall in Nearby Columbia, South Carolina. "Come on Harper, it will be fun. We can hang out, and check out the boys. I heard that the new department store has those totally-rad. new high-heel shoes in green and gold. I have to have them. Come on, please come with me."

"My mother won't let me. I'm grounded."

"I will pick you up at the end of the block. You can sneak out the back door. Come on."

"Alright."

Three months before, the City Council of Columbia, South Carolina discussed a request to increase the city's

public safety budget. Specifically, additional funds were to be allotted to security at the Apex Mall. The mall was to provide matching funds for the increased presence of security guards and monitoring systems.

The request was denied because the mayor stated that, "No funds were needed because we are Southern gentlemen and ladies. We South Carolinians fought in the Civil War, and we can protect ourselves against any terrorists who come to Columbia."

Columbia, South Carolina, the capital of the state, is a beautiful city filled with over one-hundred-thirty-five-thousand patriotic Americans. On January fifth, all of them needed to be at the Apex Mall to help fight off a terrorist attack.

The city was named after Christopher Columbus, and is a cornerstone of Richland Country. The Saluda and broad Rivers meet to form the Congaree River that flows through the city. A zoo, botanical gardens, museums, parks, world-class businesses, and statues of confederate Civil war heroes dot the city's landscape. Columbia is the essence of the Antebellum of the Old South.

The University of South Carolina has outstanding students, and their athletic teams, the "Gamecocks", have outstanding success. The largest army training base in America, Ft. Jackson, is the home to over forty thousand troops engaged in basic and advance training. The city was also one of the first planned communities in America.

The American Civil War was started in Columbia when Confederate troops under the command of P. G. T. Beauregard fired on the Union garrison at Ft. Sumter on April 12, 1861. South Carolina then seceded from the Union, and followed by Mississippi, Florida, Alabama, Georgia, Louisiana, and Texas. They were joined after the shooting started by Arkansas, Tennessee, North Carolina, and Virginia.

In 1865, Union General William Tecumseh Sherman, under his scorched earth policy, leveled the city by fire, as he made his march to the sea from Atlanta.

The city was used to being attacked, and the terror it reaped.

Libby Curtis, in a car driven by her sixteen-year-old boyfriend, Perry Drummer, parked at the end of the block and waited for Harper Kingdon. She soon exited her house, unbeknown to her mother who had grounded her, and climbed into the backseat. The three teenagers then sped to the mall.

They checked out the new shoes, and Libby completed her purchase, saying, "These are really rad Harper. You need to buy them soon." They then walked the mall, checked out the recent clothing trends, and finally decided to sit down for a soft drink at the mall food court.

They watched an old man and woman who had been married for many years enjoy a cup of coffee and pleasant conversation. The husband had a habit of touching his wife's hand as they talked, which prompted Libby to say. "Oh, how disgusting! Do you think we will do that when we're that old Harper?"

Harper made fun of the couple by saying, "No way. They are too old for that."

In the far Northeastern corner of the parking lot, a tall, dark-skinned man with black hair, eyebrows, mustache, and Fu Manchu beard and goatee, stepped out of his car, stretched his arms heavenward, turned, and took a backpack from the passenger-side front seat of the vehicle. He placed both arms, one-by-one, through the shoulder straps, and started to walk to the mall, two hundred yards ahead.

When he reached the mall he took a deep breath, entered, said a prayer in silence, and walked through the doors of the bottom floor of the mall. He had previously surveyed the site and knew exactly where he wanted to go, and if anyone would be watching him. He reached his destination near a concrete pillar that supported the upper floor of the mall.

He removed his backpack from his shoulders, and sat it down on the floor. With a quick scan, he reaffirmed that no one was near him, or had seen his movements. He knelt down, and acted like he was tightening the shoelace on the tennis shoe on his right foot.

He unzipped his backpack, flipped the on / off switch of the contents inside the bag, zipped up the backpack, stood up, then casually walked toward the exit doors of the mall, unnoticed by a single person.

When he was outside, he walked toward his car. He had walked half-way to his car when, without turning around, he took a small box that resembled a television remote control device from his pocket. He continued to walk in a Northeastern direction, then raised his head heavenward and prayed, "Glory to Allah. Please allow me the pleasure of sending these infidels to the depths of Hell." He then pushed a button on the small remote control box.

Boom! The Apex Mall exploded, sending dust, cement, insulation, steel, iron, glass, and plastic particles into the air. These elements were simultaneously joined in the atmosphere by pieces of human DNA. The man, a lone-wolf USFF supporter named Yasif El-Diz, did not turn around, and continued to walk to his car.

Once there, he unlocked the driver-side door and slid behind the steering wheel. He turned the key, put the car in D for drive, and slowly drove out the far exit of the mall. He returned to his apartment, sat in his straight, metal chair, the one that belonged with the card table, the only furniture in his apartment, and closed his eyes.

He said, "Allah will be proud of me today."

At the Apex Mall, confusion ruled the moment. Dust, fire, and horror filled the air. Many people were missing, many people were injured and waiting for help, and many were unaccounted for. First responders were arriving in a valiant attempt to save lives and bring order to the situation.

The old man and his wife were nowhere to be found. Their bodies had been blown to bits as he bomb had detonated directly under their location, on the first, not the second floor. The explosion blast had gone upward, directly into the couple's seated location. They had immediately been sent to Heaven, where they could hold hands for eternity.

Perry Drummer, Libby Curtis' boyfriend, would not be driving home from the Apex Mall, as his body parts were scattered around the rubble caused by the explosion.

Harper Kingdon would not have the opportunity to wear the shoes Libby Curtis had begged her to buy, as she too had been torn apart by the bomb blast. She would not be returning home to see her mother today, or any other day.

Libby Curtis' body was also blown apart, and lay in several locations in the rubble. A first responder dug through the debris and the rubble, and reached down to remove a large piece of concrete. He suddenly knelt down and threw up, horrified at what he had just seen.

After catching his breath, he gathered himself, reached down and moved the large piece of concrete once more, then removed a leg, with a "totally-rad", new, high-heeled, green-and-gold-colored shoe on its foot.

In City Hall, the Mayor was frantically answering phone calls and trying to make sure no other blasts were forthcoming. A member of the City Council who had opposed his ruling to shoot down the additional funds for the Apex Mall's security needs, spoke to him, "Time to resign Mayor. Terror waits for no man, especially those who are ignorant of its consequences."

Chapter 8

The Philippines

January 5

DUE TO THE DANGERS IN THE CHINA SEA AND THE actions of the "Karaoke Kid", Jun Hanuel, of North Korea, America had increased its presence in the region. Additional buildups of air and army bases had taken place near the capital of Palawan Island located near the Spratly Islands, on an island North of Luzon, on Mactan Island on the coast of Ceba in the Central Philippines, and on the Southern Island of Mindanao.

Expansion of the air base near Manila had also taken place. An agreement with the Philippine government had been executed in nineteen hundred to allow joint usage of the base between American forces and the Philippine Air Force, which controlled and owned the facilities. Operational control was augmented by the efforts a large force of civilian servants from the home country.

On January fifth, a joint-planning meeting was scheduled for Philippine and American air force leaders to address the recent increased action that, against prior negotiated and agreed upon terms, was being carried out by North Korea.

The meeting was one of high-level strategy that was to address actions to be taken if North Korea again initiated war-like actions in the China Sea. Top brass from both countries would be in attendance.

Times for the meeting were from eight a. m. to five p.m., with lunch being delivered to the base headquarters building adjacent to the parade grounds. The twelve-noon meal would consist of traditional entrees from the Philippines and America, and would be delivered by civilian workers.

At eleven a. m. the dining area was set up, with china, sterling silver knives, forks, and spoons, and traditional Philippine-style décor in the room. Food was delivered in serving dishes that would allow each person present to pass through the serving line to fill their own plate.

The atmosphere was cordial as the men and women in the meeting entered the dining room, said a prayer, filed through the line, sat down, and started to eat. Ten minutes into the meal, a Philippine civil servant from the Southernmost islands of the country named Bituin Bayani walked to the serving line with another serving dish, to supposedly refill one of the trays with more food. Bituin had grown up in the same area, Sulu Island.

The Sulu region was a safe haven, training ground, and a planning base for the CFFA. The terrorist organization sheltered fighters from Syria's USFF, the AIO, and the TCPLM. The Columbian drug cartels including the Carmelo Brothers, the Salvador Masas Mexican cartel, the Durante Sicilian mafia, the Russian SBP mafia, and was a rebel stronghold.

America had provided assistance to the Philippine people in the areas of healthcare, food, and monetary assistance, and had provided military training and weaponry to the government of the current president, Datu Laarni.

In retaliation, the CFFA had used kidnapping, armed skirmishes, terrorist acts such as bombings of government buildings and cars, disruption and terror at public and national celebrations. Laarni had responded with public trials of terrorists, airplane bombings of CFFA training camps, and a promise to "kill every terrorist in the Philippines".

Bituin was a disgruntled man as he despised the American government for their muddling in his country's affairs, and the Philippine government for their aggressive actions against his people in the Sulu region. He had lost his grandfather, father, and three older brothers in the armed conflicts in the area. He had become bitter, and determined to do something to avenge his family's losses.

He placed the large serving tray on the floor behind the tables that formed the serving line, kneeled down, said a prayer to Allah, removed the lid, took out a short-lengthened machine gun, and then two hand-grenades.

Still kneeling behind the table, he reached up, placed the two grenades on the white, cotton tablecloth, placed four magazines full of ammunition in his pockets, took the machine gun off safety, and stood up, the machine gun hanging along his right leg, on the side of his body.

He looked at the fifty-eight military people seated and eating at the table, and the seven civilian people catering to the diners' requests for more coffee, food refills, and desert requests. He scanned the room and saw that military armed guard had left his post to go to the restroom.

Knowing the coast was clear, and the moment of his revenge was at hand, Bituin yelled "Allah Akbar" and started to fire his weapon, spraying rounds across the tables where the brave military men and women were seated.

Dishes, broken glass and china plates, and blood that exploded from his victim's bodies flew through the air as men and women dropped to the floor in pain and agony. Screams and curse words filled the air as men and women attempted to dive to the floor to escape the assault, to crawl to safety, or to escape the constant barrage of firepower.

Bituin screamed obscenities as he continued firing, his hatred for the two governments, whose actions had caused the deaths of his rebel-family members who had died as freedom fighters. The scene was horrific as he continued to fire, stopping only to put new clips of ammunition in his machine gun.

When the attacker had exhausted three clips of rounds, the guard who was on duty had run from the restroom to the door of the room and had started to return fire at the assailant. Bituin wheeled and fired at the guard, his rounds riddling the doorframe the guard had ducked behind. Wood, sheetrock, and paint flew through the air as the rounds tore into the doorframe and wall.

When the attacker kneeled to reload his last clip of ammunition, the guard returned fire, sending rounds into the serving trays, mashed potatoes, rice, vegetables, coffee, milk, tablecloths, china dishes, silverware, and the tables, but not into Bituin who was safely crouched below the table.

Knowing that he was almost out of ammo, Bituin then lobbed the two hand grenades toward the military personnel. One exploded in the tables to the left of the serving line, and one tore into the center tables, instantly killing three people, and hurling shrapnel toward several other soldiers lying prone on the floor.

Bituin then screamed "Praise be Allah!", stood up and emptied his last clip of firepower. He then grabbed a large, sharp carving knife that had been used to carve meat for the meal, and rushed toward the military people on the floor near the table, fully intending to take more of them with him to the afterlife.

The armed guard at the door then fired a burst of rounds into the attacker's back, and he fell to the floor, dead before he landed.

The scene was gory, but was soon stabilized. Injured people were adhered to by medical personnel who rushed into the room. The dead were left where they had landed until the crime scene had been assessed, but were paid the respect they deserved.

The chaos had been stopped, but nine lives, six Philippine and three American military people had been lost. Six officers and three high-level enlisted personnel were dead. Five men and one woman made up the total. They had died unexpectedly, with an opportunity to fight for their lives.

In the Sulu region of the Philippines, news of the attack was reported on television. CFFA troops cheered as the reports detailed the nine deaths of their enemies, and the attack by one of their fellow freedom fighters, who was honored as a hero, a hero who was now receiving his rewards from Allah.

The CFFA freedom fighters; life was a lonely one. Living in the jungle, eating sparse food at times, dealing with bugs, snakes, and spiders, and knowing that their victories would come in small victories spread over long years of fighting might discourage some of them.

But, the majority of them would soldier on, confident that their battle for freedom who someday arrive. They would pledge their lives to make that happen.

In command headquarters, their leader sat quietly, watching the news broadcast, and thinking about the great victory that would raise the hopes of their countrymen and urge them to fight on. The leader was proud to be a CFFA fighter today, and would continue to serve to reach the destiny that had been accepted by every CFFA fighter.

After enjoying the moment, the leader assessed the life that had unfolded since joining the fight against the government. Personally, it had been costly, as a career had been abandoned, and personal goals had been discarded. A lover had also been acquired, one which was cherished more than a life as a freedom fighter.

Despite the call to duty, the lover had become increasingly more important that the military goal, an admission that the leader knew, but did not want known by the terror organization's troops.

The leader sighed, then said out loud, "I know that you know I love you. Harold Gatewood, you are the most important thing in my life, and I will soon leave the CFFA so we may have a life together."

Ligaya Diwata was at peace with herself, as she had made her decision.

Chapter 9

IOFFI

January 5

AS THE EVENTS OF TERROR WERE REPORTED ON television, Gatewood listened, then turned his thoughts to Susana Richards and the twins who would change his life forever. He wondered how she was feeling, and if she would have an easy pregnancy.

In Ireland, IOFFI leader Shamus Conti was thinking about the organization's new plans for independence. Like other struggles for independence, discrimination, bigotry, sectarian conflict, and religious, class and regional differences had impacted the IOFFI's attempts for freedom.

The story was an old one, and had been seen in Middle East with the USFF's struggle where Sharia and Sunni Muslim sects battled, in Sri Lanka, Pakistan, Japan, Africa, Australia, and the Balkans where Serbs and Croatians battled.

Ireland had been a hotbed of terrorist activities and guerrilla warfare since the raids on British landmarks, towns, and forts since the seventeen hundreds. The Irish Citizen Army resisted their Irish brothers who fought against Germany, the British army, and the Royal Ulster Constabulary in the Irish War for Independence in 1920.

Conflicts from trade union wars in Ireland also led to riots, and the establishment of resistance movement-minded Irish patriots who eventually demanded independence for Northern Ireland from the United Kingdom. The roots of the organizations were founded in a desire for free socialist republic, home rule, and the end of British control. Political violence to attain their goals was the watchword of their day.

Treaties were signed and broken, followed by terrorist acts such as car bombings, kidnappings, and murders of members of the British government. Recent Events had led to an unsuccessful vote to leave the United Kingdom, which fueled the anger of the current terrorist group, Irish Order of Workers For Freedom and Independence, the IOWFFI.

The organization was led by military head Alastar Cowal, and governed by a seven-member war council that had military and political arms.

The recent illegal immigration invasion of England further angered the IOWFFI, as they did not relate to the spill-over of Syrian people that had taken over London. The Northern Irish freedom fighters did not understand the lifestyle of the Middle Eastern hordes of "invaders" into Great Britain and wanted to immediately distance themselves from the trend they saw as dangerous to Irish Independence.

The IOWFFI identified itself with the AIO in Spain and the TCPLM in Columbia. The all shared weaponry and technology that made their quest for freedom easier. The AIO was providing C4 explosive to the Northern Irish patriots, and the TCPLM was providing drugs that the IOWFFI sold, and used the proceeds from, to buy weaponry.

The three-way cooperation between the groups was now causing a continuous stream of problems for Great Britain. The IOWFFI sent fighters to Columbia to train the TCPLM soldiers in terrorist street- fighting tactics, and in return for weapons and drugs.

The AIO and the IOWFFI each exchanged paramilitary terror tactics. The AIO had fought for their independence and a Basque homeland since the Roman times. Their area of operation included almost all of Spain, in the Vizcaya, Gipuzkoa, Alava, and some of the Navarra regions.

The areas in France included the three Southern provinces, Basse-Navarre, Lahourd, and Soule, all located near the ocean and the hills near the Pyrenees mountains.

The IOWFFI and the AIO exchanged proficiencies in kidnapping politicians and wealthy businessmen, car bombing, and assassination attempts on each country's leaders. The IOWFFI was considered the world's best at constructing bombs. Skills were passed from one person to the next in an elaborate, detailed training program, which took years to master.

The Northern Ireland freedom fighters did not want to use bombings that caused mass casualties. Instead, they targeted troops, police, and political figures in London, Belfast, and Dublin. Their long and bloody campaign was designed to bring England to the bargaining table to meet the organization's demands for freedom.

They had occasionally used trucks loaded with over three thousand pounds of IED's and explosives to hit a large city target, but they preferred to use their wit and bravery to plant smaller level of explosives to make statements and create public fear. Nuclear, biological, and chemical weapons, as well as a weapon of mass destruction were also in their arsenal, but were not their weapons of choice.

Adaptability, flexibility, and a constant change of approach had led to success for the IOWFFI for years and they were loyal to that approach. New threats were always presented, ones which kept the British busy developing "bomb-proof" vehicles, robots to disarm bombs, and stronger HUMIT human intelligence abilities to ferret out possible attacks.

Even in Gatewood's father's days in England, the Northern Irish freedom fighters were trying to kill Winston Churchill, MI5 members, police, and security forces. While the British were content to remove spies and "moles" inside their government operations, the IOWFFI preferred to kill any traitors they uncovered.

The recent event in London had led to a large stockpiling of bombs, handguns, assault rifles, submachine guns, rocket launchers, flamethrowers, Semtex and C4 explosives, truck-mounted mortars, and surface-to-air-missiles to be used against British security forces.

Conri closed his eyes and thought as dates and names passed through his memories about the IOFFI's struggle for independence. The Anglo-Irish Treaty of 1922, Michael Collins and the Civil War of 1922 and 3, the Fianna Fail Party of 1932, the 1969 Loyalist attack on Northern Ireland and the resulting riots, Bloody Sunday in 1972, the Sunningdale Agreement and a new Parliment in 1973, the 1981 hunger strike where ten political prisoners died, and the 1993 downing Street Declaration.

He thought, "We made progress but the struggled did not stop."

He then recounted further events, the Tiger economy and progress of the mid-nineteen nineties, Sinn Fein and Gary Adams and the ceasefire in 1994, the new Northern Ireland Assembly and full Irish power in 1998, the bombing in Omagh later in 1998, the second ceasefire in 2005, the 2007 resumption of the north Ireland Assembly, the 2008 Irish banking system bankruptcy and failure, and the 2010 bailout to put Ireland on its feet again.

Conri then said, "It is now time to fight again."

Chapter 10

WISAM

January 5

IN WALES, EINION CRYFDER, LEADER OF THE Welsh Independent Sovereignty Alliance Movement, thought about the need for a free Welsh country. Wales was located in the Northwestern area of Great Britain. The struggle for independence had taken place since the Norman Invasion and rule, and since 1282 when Edward I of England was conquered.

The current demand for Welsh independence was supported by the political leadership, advisory groups, the public, and had intensified with England's recent decision to flee their partnership with the other countries in Europe.

If nationalism was good for the goose, England, then it was good for the gander, Wales. The Welsh Independent Sovereignty Alliance Movement, WISAM, was ready for independence, and Einion Cryfder, the "Anvil of Strength", was ready to lead the fight,

The organization's demands included independence and self-determination, full ownership of the area's oil and gas natural resources, freedom from the high taxes piled on them by England, freedom to enjoy the cultural growth and pride in the Welsh heritage, and the protest

of the protest of the takeover of England by the illegal immigrants an terrorists affiliated with the USFF.

Cryfder laughed at the thought that the same "taxation without representation" demand that America had desired in its Revolutionary War, was now being repeated in Wales. Current day England was ignoring and failing Wales the same as it had done to America prior to its own war for independence.

From Cardiff, the capital of Wales, to its borders, the country wanted freedom, jobs, better economic opportunity, and to free itself from England's constant siphoning out of the country's resources and national pride. Einion Cryfder and the WISAM were the tip of the spear that was pointed at England, demanding its first birthday as a free nation.

Cryder thought about the road to independence that all captive satellite colonies needed to travel to become free nations. He said, "Perhaps it is true, one man's terrorist is another man's freedom fighter." I am the spear head of the Welsh movement, and I will battle Great Britain to the death to lead my countrymen to freedom.

"We have waited too long for our independence, and we will not be stopped by actions in London. We are Welshmen, not Englishmen. Like the AIO in Spain, we have tried peaceful negotiations I the past, to no avail. Now we will use any means necessary to break from our master. We will be serfs and beggars no more. It is time for action, and action we will bring. Great Britain has stomped on our efforts to be free, and has clouded and dictated our future from London. We have reached our limit, and will endure no more of these heinous actions.

We are Welshmen, and we will be free. Great Britain be dammed."

Chapter 11

SPFIF

January 5

IN EDINBURG, THE CAPITAL OF SCOTLAND, THE leader of the Scottish Patriots For Independence And Freedom, Conall Blair, the Strong Wolf Of The Battlefield", took stock of his beloved country of Scotland.

From his early childhood Blair had become lost in the beauty of Scotland. He had been born in Inverness in the Scottish Highlands of the North. As a young boy his parents had taken him to Loch Ness to try to spot "Nessie", the infamous monster of Loch Ness. His family had moved to Glasgow on the opposite coast of the country when he was fourteen, where he appreciated the lowlands.

The landscape of the country was bathed in a beautiful green color, and was surrounded by the blue and gray waters of the North Sea off the coast of Edinburg, the, and the Atlantic Ocean off the coast of Glasgow. Blair loved the rugged, colorful stories about the country's history, and the laid-back nature of its people.

Three-fourths of the country's five million people lived in the lowlands. The Roman name for the country was Caledonia, and the Galic name was Alba. The Irish lifestyle was tied to the sea and its bounties. The Highlands were mostly people who were often found dressed in kilts, and worshiped the Catholic faith, while the Protestant faith was predominant in the Lowlands.

Food was basic, with potatoes and turnips, called "neeps and talties", a fish soup made of haddock called "Cullen skink", meat pies called "brides", and the national dish of the heart, liver, and lungs cooked in the animal's stomach, and mixed with oatmeal and spices. It took a true Scottish citizen to eat the dish, called "haggis".

Another national tradition was the downing of Scottish whisky, which was distilled twice, as opposed to Irish Whiskey, which was spelled differently, and distilled three times before it was enjoyed. Both rivaled the famous "Vanducci whisky" of Fabbri Durante's Sicily. The country citizenry also enjoyed soccer, and claimed to have invented the sport of golf.

Blair was captivated by the country's famous figures like Sir Walter Scott, Rob Roy, Robert Louis Stevenson, Robert Burns, Robert The Bruce, and William Wallace, who defeated English King Edward I, called Longshanks, in Scotland's earlier bid for freedom and independence.

Blair's grandfather and father had worked in the SPFIF, and had passed the fierce passion for independence at any cost to Conall at his early age of four, and it had grown in intensity ever since.

The Westphalia model, where each nation-state had its own self-rule, did not exist in Scotland, and it was in the same growing process as Northern Ireland and Wales. The Kurds in Iraq, the AIO in Spain and Southern France, and even Eric Clancy's nationalistic-centered election in America also shared the same desire for nationalism. Globalism was facing daunting challenge.

The latest Scottish attempt at independence, a peaceful one at the ballot box, had been headed by Conall Blair, and his Scottish Patriots For Independence And Freedom, the SPFIF. Prior votes for independence had been defeated by promises from England to give more self-rule for Scotland, all of which had remained undelivered.

The SPFIF failed politically to deliver independence. Now, Blair and his organization sensed it was time to act, either politically, or para-militarily, once again. Scottish citizens had had enough of Great Britain's rule, and wanted a change.

Like Wales, Scotland had also been a pality, a faction within a larger entity, England, since the Middle Ages. The fires of patriotism were again burning in the hearts of Scottish citizens, all of whom wanted to shed the centuries-old English yoke around their necks.

Connal Blair had convinced his paramilitary leaders that violence should become the norm for the independence movement, and it should start immediately. The SPFIF held a huge war chest and had doled out many dollars to buy weapons and ammunition from Yua Hayato's Yakaza crime family. The weaponry would soon arrive on Scottish shores, and the membership would put it to good use against the Scottish loyalists to Great Britain, and the British troops that would be sent to Scotland.

Training had taken place in Northern Ireland by the IOFFI, who was also plotting paramilitary action against Great Britain. Soon, the cities, police and military forces, and citizens of England would feel the wrath of the SPFIF, IOFFI, and the WISAM.

Blair thought, "From the beautiful mountainous region's highest point in the country on Ben Nevis of the Scottish Highlands, to Inverness, to the Glencoe Valley, to the pine forests, to the lowlands, we will fight. William Wallace led us to victory at the Battle of Stirling Bridge, and Robert the Bruce continued the fight. I will lead Scotland in its new fight for independence and freedom.

England will feel the sting that is foretold in our motto on our coat of arms, 'Nemo me impune lacessit', which means 'No one provokes me without impunity.' Blair then pounded his fist on his desk and said, 'Truly free Scotland now!'"

Chapter 12

Set To Explode

January 7

IT HAD BEEN LESS THAN A WEEK AGO WHEN Susana Richards had shocked Gatewood with the news that she was pregnant and he was going to become a father. She had then surprised him further when she had told him that she was going to have two babies.

He had been knocked off his feet with the news, especially when he had heard that twins would be arriving. He knew that his life was not only going to change, but that the experience would be a new, uncharted voyage into parenthood. He knew that his parents would be shocked, and overjoyed, as they had wanted grandchildren, and had come to the realization that it would never happen.

He laughed when he thought of how his mom would find the tiny baseball uniform that she had made for him when he was born and have it ready for one of the twins. He knew she would start sewing a second uniform for the second twin as soon as she heard the news.

His dad would also be busy, looking for a tiny gloves and baseball bats that would be gifts as soon as they were born. Harold remembered his childhood and how much time he had spent with his dad learning the game. It would be fun to go through that experience again with his two boys.

He called Susana to see how she was feeling and to give her more encouragement that he was overjoyed with the news, and that the more he had thought about it, he had wondered why they had not been blessed with the event earlier.

She was lying down, resting, when he called. She was happy to hear his voice and gushed with joy when he told her how much he loved her, and the two babies who would make their appearance in a few months. She had not had any morning sickness, but knew that her body was changing. She hoped that she would have an easy pregnancy, as her mother had not had one when Susana was born.

They talked about the program her doctor would have her follow, and when they would get together again. She had a contract hit scheduled in the near future, and would take other assignments as long as she felt well enough to do the dangerous work that had become her calling. They closed the call with "1 love you's", and with smiles on their faces.

After the call ended, Harold sat in his chair by the window and looked at his friends the squirrels dig up food they had stored for the Winter, and then take it to the tree. The birds had flown South for the Winter and would no doubt be gathering food there, Their acts struck home with him, as he would soon be doing somethings similar in nature for his new family. He smiled, as he knew that fatherhood would agree with him.

His pleasant mood was interrupted by a phone call. Rick Owens spoke, "Harold, Happy New Year! How are you?"

Without telling Owens why, he said, "I am really doing great Rick. How are you?"

"I am fine Harold. Are you available to come to Washington this week? I have a mission that requires your special skills."

"Yes, I need to get out of here. When do you want me there?"

"Can you leave tomorrow? Then we can talk, two days from now."

The next day Gatewood was on his flight to Washington, sitting in seat 3A on both segments of his trip. He wondered what Owens wanted, but he knew that it was important, based on the urgency of Owens' request that he arrive almost immediately. Harold also knew that, somehow, he had already developed a connection to the assignment.

While his thought was correct, it did not narrow down the possibilities, as he had unfinished business with the AIO, the Columbian and Mexican drug cartels, the Durante Mafia in Sicily, the TCPLM and the government in Venezuela, the OWFA, and the corrupt organization of Mayor Riccardo Gennaro in Chicago.he had learned long ago that enemies, old and new, would be waiting for him, and trying to guess which one would encompass his mission, would be hopeless.

After arriving, he checked into his hotel room, number one hundred, unpacked, worked out in the fitness center, enjoyed the swimming pool and the steam bath, ate supper, and then slept through the night, free of nightmares. The next morning he headed to CIO headquarters, announced himself at the front desk, and sat down in the lobby.

After a ten minute wait, he was joined by Sahara Aziz, the attractive young lady who had escorted him to Rick Owens' office in the past. As they walked, and then rode the elevator upstairs, Sahara was her usual talkative self, again asking him what he considered to be prying questions about his presence in CIO headquarters.

She asked, "Are you here for a mission Mr. Gatewood? Where are they sending you this time? How long will you be gone? Will it be dangerous? Who will you be meeting?"

Gatewood chalked up Sahara's improper interest to that of a young girl who did not understand the sensitive nature of the espionage business. When they reached Owens' floor, they exited the elevator and walked past an office that had recently be moved to its current location.

Harold noticed that a young man had looked out at them, and appeared to look at Sahara, as if acknowledging her. He did not know that the man was Tayeb Rizwan, Sahara's lover, and fellow USFF spy.

Gatewood continue on to Owens' office, said hello to Owens' secretary Loretta Owens, thanked Sahara Aziz for the assistance in reaching the office, and had a seat. While Harold waited for Owens, Loretta Owens and he talked about her mother, and how she was feeling.

"She is making the best of it. She is very sick. At least she is now in the best care unit in the city. It is very expensive, but I want to make sure she has the best treatment possible."

Gatewood wondered about how a secretary could afford the best, and most expensive, treatment center in the area. Loretta had told him previously that her mother was not wealthy and paying for her care was talking all of her mother's assets. Loretta had also moved her mother from a less-quality, lower cost facility to the current location. Something did not add up, but Gatewood did not say anything.

Owens came to his office door and motioned for Harold to come in and sit down. Once inside he said, "Welcome Harold. It is nice to see you again. I did not think that you would be back here this soon, but events have changed."

Gatewood said that he was happy to be back, and then Owens, Terry Robbins, and he got down to business.

Harold asked, "What is happening Rick?"

"Harold, in the last two weeks a great deal of terrorist activity has taken place. We have been monitoring those events, and other situations that are developing."

"Yes, I saw some of the recent events on television."

"Harold, several situations are ready to explode. Let's move on and address what is happening in Europe. As we have discussed before, the illegal immigrant invasion from the Middle East has altered Europe forever. Germany is now suffering from their ill-fated decision to welcome all immigrants at the expense of their national interests."

"Yes, they were the first to do so."

Owens had then continued, "Yes. They needed to reboot their population as their birth rate was falling, and in a few years they would need more people to man their economy. But, the decision has been taken at the expense of their culture. Now the German people are upset, angry, and want to reverse the decisions of their leader."

"Yes. She lost the election and is out. The new man in charge will have to clean up her mess."

"True, but it will be difficult, and take time. They now face the influx of immigrants who do not want to assimilate into the German culture, and want to impose their own beliefs on the country."

"It is no wonder the German citizenry is upset."

"Yes. The country's social institutions are breaking down. The country now has to deal with terrorists who want to create havoc. They will need to put a cap on immigration or continue to decline. Many USFF fighters have entered the country and are poised to strike."

"What have they done to shore up their security?"

Owens had then answered, "They are using good tactics, and the German people seem to have the resolve to help address the problems. If the politicians will keep a stiff backbone then there will be progress. If not, then kiss Germany goodbye."

Robbins added, "I agree Sir"

"Spain continues to face their economic and internal terrorist problems. The AIO is still operating. In fact, they just announced thy plan to hold their own, unsanctioned elections to declare independence from Spain and Southern France. We know they have sent operatives to train with the TCPLM in Columbia."

Owens had continued, "We also know that they are beefing up the number of their agents in order to forcibly attempt to gain independence for their members if their election is unsuccessful. They are on the move again."

"What is being done in opposition to the AIO?"

"King Alfonso IV has given his full support to fight the resistance forces. He was also very pleased that you did a little favor for him when you was last in Venezuela."

Robbins stated, "He is a good ally for America."

"Yes he is. We have urged Spain to stop the immigration from Greece, which has tripled recently, as more illegals are coming by sea."

Owens continued, "In England, the people voted to leave the common market and stand for their national unity. They have faced more terrorist problems due to the changing complexion of their population. They used to be our strongest partner in Europe. Harold, there has been an average of one terror attack every six days in Europe, Illegal immigration has been so bad in London that the city is now called Londinistan."

"I agree Rick. Terrorism is still rising there."

"France has been rocked with terrorist attacks. They have a severe problem on their hands. Terrorist groups have them in their sights and have threatened many more attacks. They recently escaped a tragedy when Gatewood helped stop the USFF from exploding a pope sale, a dirty bomb, in Paris. But, immigrants from Africa are now pouting into the country."

"Sir, they have recognized that they are a target and have been forced to deal with the problem.

"Yes, with help from the world community they may be able to keep that situation under control."

Owens replied, "The same situation exists in Belgium. They have been hit hard in Brussels on multiple occasions. They are now taking the problem very seriously."

"Yes, they were unprepared before they were hit."

"Switzerland is now being affected by terrorism. They have refused to take immigrants. But, they are in several terrorist groups' takeover plans. The leaders of the country say that immigration will continue to overrun Europe until a change of policy is made."

"They are pretty isolated."

"True, but they only have a volunteer civil defense plan, and have no military."

"They would be prime target if the country were infiltrated."

Owens had then continued on the European rundown. "The intelligent European countries have closed down their borders, and are not allowing illegal immigrants to enter. If they can keep out the illegals they will be okay. Hungary and Poland have been resistant to taking any immigrants, and have not suffered an attack."

Owens then addressed the fact that immigration had led to increased terrorism. "Bavaria has stated that immigration will not be slowed down, and increased terrorism will continue. Immigrants come from Albania to Bulgaria to London, which is now completely overrun with illegals. Boatloads of illegals arrive by sea in Spain.

"They will be one of the few countries who will be attack-free."

"Italy is now being impacted on an even higher level. Even Lake Como has illegals housed near the town. It has come out that the Durante mafia is making money off of the immigration situation, especially those from the Libyan route into the country. Italy is now deporting more and more terrorists, including the migrants from North Africa, as soon as they arrive, and has announced a zero tolerance policy on immigration.

They have now closed their borders and no immigrants are accepted from the non-Italian boats and ships that have been dropping off immigrants. They are sending the illegals Northward. The disappointing fact is that now the Durante mafia is cooperating with the illegals in the prostitution and drug trade."

Harold answered, "I am sure that is causing a response from the rich and famous people who live there. I saw where Austria and Greece are now also refusing to accept immigrants in their countries. Austria's leader said that illegal immigrants will overtake the European continent in the next few years."

"Yes it is. Europe has lost it culture, and traditions. They are even failing to pay their fair share for protection and are proving to be a failing group of partners in our treaty agreements."

"What is happening in Ireland?"

"The Irish independence gang has again started making bombs so it looks like Ireland will develop into a hot spot again. It has really heated up in the last two weeks"

Gatewood asked, "What about Sweden and Finland?"

Owens had then answered, "They are now experiencing problems from illegals they allowed in their country. There have been many attacks and rapes of Swedish women who have been going about their everyday life. I am sure you saw what happened this week when the townspeople acted as vigilantes to attack the immigrants who raped a young girl."

Yes, I did see that Rick. What about the rest of that
area of the world?"

"It will continue to have problems if they admit illegals. Finland has also been hurt in the same manner as Sweden. They are too liberal for their own good."

"Hopefully, they have learned their lesson."

"Harold, I want to also bring you up to date on matters that arose during your recent mission in Rome."

"What has taken place?"

"We have determined that you were correct in thinking that the Durante mafia from Palermo, Sicily, the Carmelo cartel from Columbia, the TCPLM, and the Masas cartel from Mexico are working with the Catholic Church in the Vatican."

Gatewood replied, "They are going on an all-out blitz to bring illegal immigrant to Italy, disperse them through Europe, hook them on drugs, and partner with them to push drugs and prostitution."

"Exactly. And the Vatican is taking a cut of fees that the immigrants are charged for passage to Italy. Also, they are paid a per-head fee by the humanitarian world organizations for each immigrant they help settle in Europe. They are getting paid twice for each immigrant they help settle in Europe."

"That is what I feared Rick. What about the Pope?"

"He is happy to take the money from the immigrants, who are mostly Muslim worshipers."

"Rick, is the Pope being targeted for assassination?"

"Yes. The USFF, and their splinter groups such as the CFFA, are planning to kill him. You did a great job in Italy, and your information helped us notice the phone and email traffic from the terror organizations that led us to that conclusion."

Gatewood thought about his mission in Rome, and how he had uncovered the information that had led to the CIO gaining the valuable information Owens had just mentioned.

After Gatewood had decided to enter the grounds of the Vatican, he had been surrounded by several thousand tourists. He had watched them tour the grounds of the walled city-state, taking in the museums, art works, elegant architecture, and St. Peter's Basilica. While he had seen tourists of many stripes and variations, he did not spot any suspicious plots afoot over four days of sitting in St. Peter's Square.

While staking out the personal residence of the Pope, he had noticed the Gendarmerie Corps of the Vatican City, the police and security forces of the city-state. The one-hundred-thirty-member force was armed with semi-automatic machine guns, and nine millimeter pistols to ensure riot control, and protection for the Pope.

Security measures at the entry gate were organized, well-fortified, and efficient, and appeared to be more than required to prevent terrorist weapons to be smuggled into the walled area of the Vatican. Backpacks were inspected and scanned and tourists were required to walk through a full-body scanning machine similar to those used in American airports.

Gatewood had been impressed with the security measures. He had been more interested to see if the pope would have any official visitors that might reveal any political or "shady" possible relationships that might lead the Pope into danger, or shed light on any possible dealings that might harm American interests.

After he had personally walked the grounds, and getting a view of the situation firsthand, he returned to his surveillance through his binoculars in his hotel room.

Gianna Sabina had stopped by his room late in the afternoon, and gave him a perfect opportunity to give his weary eyeballs, bleak from hours of glassing the Vatican grounds, a break from his surveillance. They had made love, then laid in bed talking about their day, and their strong feelings for each other.

After two hours, they had showered together, and dressed for a light supper at the nearby restaurant that had become their favorite eatery. While she finished combing her beautiful, long red hair in front of the bathroom mirror, he had walked to his binoculars to take another look at the pope's personal residence.

His eyes had dilated and he had been shocked to see two men being escorted through the front door of the papal residence. One was Morte Improvvisa, the Durante family killer that had been waiting for a long time to inflict death on Gatewood, and the other was the man himself, Fabbri Durante.

Gatewood had succeeded in the first goal of his mission, spotting what the CIO had asked him to check for, the meeting between Durante and the pontiff, and was overjoyed. He had been happy that Gianna, still combing her hair and putting on the finishing touches of her makeup, would require a few more minutes to get ready for supper. He had watched the front gate of the residence for five more minutes and then headed to supper with his Italian countess lover.

Over the next three days, he had watched Durante and his bodyguard, Morte Improvvisa, arrive late in the afternoon, enter, and stay for approximately thirty minutes, then leave. The CIO had briefed him about the possibility that Durante and the Pope might meet to discuss the possibility of the church applying additional pressure on the Italian government to change its policy about not allowing the illegal immigrants Durante was dumping on the Italian shores to stay in the country.

The church had humanitarian reasons for allowing the illegal immigrants to stay in Italy. But, the CIO thought that there were financial reasons as well. The CIO was sure that Durante and the church were splitting some of the thousands of dollars they were charging each illegal immigrant for passage to Italy with the church.

The partnership would bring countless dollars into the church, and the CIO felt that the Pope would be more than willing to take money from the Muslim illegals to fund Christian projects and goals. It would be a partnership made and implemented by the devil, but it had not been the first such deal that had ever been struck.

Ex-American President Lance Edwards had worked with the Middle Eastern countries to flood America with Muslim-worshiping immigrants and dealt with North Korea and Iran on unholy deals that had threatened American security.

Gatewood had called Rick Owens to inform him of his findings, and his suspicion that he would find out additional information that would be useful. He also had a personal reason for his request that he stay on indefinitely in Rome, as he did not want to leave Gianna Sabina.

He said, "Rick, my trip to the British Isles has to wait. Something big is brewing here in Rome."

Owens spoke, "Harold, did you hear me?"

Gatewood said, "I am sorry Rick, I was thinking how I obtained the information you were speaking about. What did you ask me?"

"I said, do you have any questions?"

"Yes I do. Do you have any information about Salvador Masas?"

"He is back in Mexico doing his evil deeds. We are happy to find out he is also involved with the other cartels in the drug blitz in Europe. It may give us another chance to kill him."

"I would like that mission Rick. What about Rafael and Edwardo Carmelo?"

"As we spoke, they are in on the plot. They are now rivaling the Masas cartel for the infamy of being the largest cartel in the world."

"What about Natalio Vicent and the TCPLM?"

"They are gearing up for the Europe drug blitz also. Despite the massive problems in Venezuela, they are now shipping more drugs for the cartels than ever before. Venezuela is hanging on by a thread, and will soon put in another narco-state President to keep the status quo for the cartels."

"What are we doing about the situation with the Pope?"

"We are monitoring the Vatican. He is weak and sick, and has cancelled all of his trips for at least six months, barring a strong comeback to good health. We may need you for that detail in the future."

"I thought that would be where you are sending me now."

"No. We have another assignment for you. We will talk about that in a minute."

"What about Fabbri Durante?"

"He is not going anywhere for a while, as his work in Europe will keep his very busy."

"Rick, what about Gianna Sabina?"

"She has dropped off the radar screen. We think she killed Morte Improvissa to protect you because she loved you. We think she is an OWFA agent."

"I understand. She deceived me, but at least she saved my life."

"Harold, do you want to hear about your mission?"

"Of course."

"Nationalism is on the march, much to the displeasure of the OWFA. The British Isles are about to explode in conflict. Ireland, Scotland, and Wales are all gearing up for terrorism against Great Britain. They are buying guns and ammunition, and have been stockpiling explosives. They will act soon if England does not allow them complete, real independence, and let them cut all ties with the mother country."

"Are they capable of creating havoc and succeeding in reaching their goals?"

"Yes. The anti-England sentiment has been there for centuries and it is ready to blow up again. This time, the citizenry is almost one hundred percent supportive in the action."

"Where are they getting their weapons Rick?"

"We think that the Chechens and the Ukrainians are supplying them. Plus, there is one additional source we have not identified as of yet."

Gatewood did not say anything, but in his mind, he thought, "Chicago. Gennaro's gun-running operation may be the other source. And, Yua Hyato might be the provider, the same as they are for Japan. Oh no."

Owens continued, "Harold we want you to make the rounds and speak with the leaders of the movement in Ireland, Scotland, and Wales. Uncover what you can and then head to London to speak with their political leaders."

"How bad is the situation?"

"It is very bad. England, and especially London, has sold their heritage to allow illegal immigrants, mainly those who worship Islam, to take over the city and the country. Terror happens weekly, if not daily, and the government is losing control.

The country is losing its soul, and may not have the desire, or capability, to stop the internal takeover. That situation may render them impotent to handle the problems in Ireland, Scotland, and Wales. Their plate is full right now."

"When would I leave?"

"Immediately, if you can. If not, within a week."

"I need to go back home, make some business and personal arrangements, and then I can leave within the week Rick."

"That is great Harold. You will be centering in Ireland, as they are already up to speed in the terror department. You can then go to Scotland and wales as needed. The islands are small and transportation between them is very good."

"How long will I be there?"

"We don't know. You will then go to London. You may be shuttling back and forth after you lay the groundwork for the mission."

"I understand."

"Harold, be careful. There is danger, as you will be dealing with terror groups who have a long-standing grudge against England. In London, you need to be very careful, as the USFF is very strong there. Watch your back."

"Thank you Rick. I will."

After Gatewood had left, and the work day had ended, Loretta Walters made several phone calls, providing the information about Gatewood's mission. After passing the information, she said, "I will need another ten thousand dollars on top of my regular fee, as this mission will give you a great opportunity to kill Gatewood."

A voice on the other end of the phone said, "Agreed."

In their apartment, Sahara Aziz smiled at her boyfriend Tayeb Rizwan, then made a call to her superiors. "I saw Gatewood today, and thanks to the bug we placed in Loretta Walters' apartment, we know that Gatewood will head to the British Isles within the week, and will be there for an undetermined period of time. This will be an excellent opportunity to kill him."

A voice on the other end of the phone said, "Good work Sahara. You and Tayeb will be compensated for the information."

Sahara smiled at Tayeb, clicked off her cellphone, walked to him, took has arm, led him to the bedroom, and said, "Everything is working out as planned darling."

Chapter 13

Talpidae

January 8

MOLES LIVING IN NORTH AMERICA ARE CLASSIFIED as members of the Talpidae family. They are small, live a subterranean lifestyle, are pests, avoid each other, and burrow underground for food.

"Moles" planted inside the American government also live a subterranean lifestyle to keep their illegal activities hidden, were pests to the American people, have to avoid their co-harts to prevent detection, and burrow into the depths of American files to gain information that would be useful to harm America. Moles could be foreign enemy agents, or domestic threats from citizens inside the country.

On the foreign side of the equation, the USFF had been very successful in planting moles inside the CIO. The leader of the North American Council for Allah, NACO, inside the USFF, Ala Al-Din, had placed Aamir Jawdat inside the CIO's innermost foreign affairs area related to Syria and the Middle East.

Jawdat had operated unseen by the CIO until Director Rick Owens had seen him picking up a message under a rock on the running track in their neighborhood. Since Jawdat was not athletic, and had new walking workout clothes and tennis shoes that never seemed to wear out or get dirty, Owens' suspicions had arisen. Surveillance on Jawdat had led to the identification of his go-between for files and discs of information about CIO missions that were then funneled to his contact near Washington.

Aamir, his wife Bahiyya, and his go-between Duha Dua, were later tailed by CIO agent Jack Taylor, were all arrested and imprisoned. Information obtained by Taylor helped lead to the arrest of more USFF spies, and to increased attacks on USFF training camps near Washington, D. C., and the Southwestern border of the United States.

The CIO attack and joint mission with Mexican authorities, put USFF operative Abd Al-Qadir in prison, and prevented the detonation of a dirty bomb at a power plant near Phoenix, Arizona. Follow-up plots in Paris, France to blow up the Louvre Museum and a shootout in the Chicago, Illinois airport to kill Harold Gatewood were a result of the USFF's feud that had developed from Jawdat's efforts and information.

The USFF had successfully placed an agent, now-deceased, ex-president Lance Edwards and his lover and Chief of Staff Govad Zal, at the highest level of the American government. The result was an unholy alliance between Lance Edwards and the USFF that compromised the national security of the United States.

"Moles" in the government pose serious dangers indeed.

Moles who can pose threats can also be domestic in nature. The Manhattan Project in Los Alamos, New Mexico during World War II was a race to develop an atomic bomb that America could use to end the war, or that Hitler's Germany could use to gain world domination.

Information was at a premium, and countries whose interests were in opposition to America were willing to pay for it in order to advance their evil agenda. One such country found two willing sellers in Julius and Ethel Rosenberg, who were found guilty of section 2 of the Espionage Act for providing information to Russia.

They were executed on June 9, 1953 at Sing Sing prison in Ossining, New York.

Death in the electric chair heated their body and blood and caused ventricular fibrillation. As the electric current passed through their bodies their skin, muscles, and heat heated and singed. Their hearts quivered and stopped pumping blood to their brains and cardiac arrest took place. They were then officially declared dead.

America had had a long list of traitors in its history. The CIO top ten list of such people included benedict Arnold in the Revolutionary War, Vice-President Aaron Burr in the Thomas Jefferson administration, Iva Toguri D'Aquino who served as Japan's "Tokyo Rose" during World War II.

They were joined by American double agents Robert Hansen and Aldrich Ames who fed information to Russia. In the Civil War, an American military tribunal delivered guilty pleas and hung Lewis Powell, David Herold, George Atzerodt, and Mary Surratt. They also found Sam Arnold, Michael O'Laughlen, and Doctor Samuel Mudd guilty in the plot that led to the death of President Abraham Lincoln and sentenced them to life in prison.

John Surratt was tried and found not guilty for his role in the plot. Assassin John Wilkes booth was killed as he attempted to escape to the South.

Treason was defined as the act of betraying America and trying to kill its sovereign leader or overthrow its government. Symptoms included treachery, disloyalty, faithlessness sedition, mutiny, rebellion, and a lese-majiste, a violation of the dignity of the nation's leader.

Sedition was defined further in an amendment in 1918 to the Sedition Act as conduct or speech or organization to incite the people rebel against the authority of America or its leader.

As ex-president Lance Edwards and Govad Zal worked the same as Mary Surratt, in their "nest where the actions and plots were hatched" to undermine and overthrow the Eric Clancy Presidency and replace it with their own, they had continued their crimes against America. Their approach was "personal gain first, ideology second, and America last".

Their actions against America had continued in and out of office. They were treading on dangerous ground but still felt immune to America's laws. After all, they had operated inside and outside of America's laws for the eight years of their tenure in office. Why should they stop now? They had made great strides in advancing their agenda and in tearing down American institutions, heritages, culture, and its Constitution.

Yes, they felt entitled, and untouchable. Soon, their fate might be decided by the American Constitution, the same document whose principles they had spat on and trampled on for eight years.

"Moles" can create serious dangers and create devastating damages. Now, there were new dangers being created by the three current moles in the CIO. Foreign moles Sahara Aziz and her analyst boyfriend Tayeb Rizwan were feeding information to the USFF that would endanger the life of the Pope of the Catholic Church. Domestic mole Loretta Walters was doing likewise for many other terrorist organizations.

All of the moles' actions were also endangering the life of Harold Gatewood.

Chapter 14

To London

January 9

ALA Al-DIN, LEADER OF THE NORTH AMERICAN Council for Allah, the NACA, looked at his fellow councilmembers and spoke in a determined voice.

"My fellow USSF co-harts, tonight we will review the events of the past failed endeavor and then discuss a bold, dangerous, new mission we are going to take to avenge our recent failures. We are going to make a statement in the name of Allah that will bring honor to his name, and that will also show the weakness of those who oppose our beliefs."

Al-Din's comments were met with approval by the council, and he then started his review of the past failed missions in Washington, D.C., the training camp on the American-Mexican border, in Paris, France, and at the airport in Chicago, Illinois.

"My fellow believers, we know the following from our moles Susana Aziz and Tayeb Rizwan who have been placed inside the CIO. The British Isles are about to be set on fire by new drives for independence and freedom from England by Ireland, Scotland, and Wales.

These actions will cause more confusion, and turmoil, for the English government and allow us to further strengthen our foothold in London. As we all know, we have just succeed in electing the first Mayor of London who worships Islam. This situation will also allow us to increase our terrorist attacks on London and other major cities in England."

Questions were raised by the council members about the mission.

"The terrorist events that will break out in Ireland, Scotland, and Wales by the actions of the IOFFI, SPFIF, and the WISAM will help sap the strength of the British government. When they can't keep the lid on the problem they will try to use force to quell the rebellions. The result will be the exodus of Ireland, Scotland, and Wales, and the further weakening of England.

We will then create additional problems from within the city of London that will further cripple the government. England will start collapsing in the cities and in the country. They will have more than they can handle, which combined with our continuing flood of immigration will lead to gains in power for us.

Also, we know that Gatewood will be working for the CIO with the three rebellious areas and with the English government in London. He will be a sitting duck and will can easily kill him.

I have handpicked one of our best operatives, Halim Rasul, to spearhead our mission in London. His name means "patient and tolerant", and his is just that. He will wait until the perfect time to kill Gatewood. I have also tapped him to handle the devastating terror attack I have planned for London. He will choose two fellow USFF operatives to assist him in the terror attack and the disposal of Harold Gatewood.

Our fellow believer who heads 'our favorite masque in London', Tabassum Marham, will provide shelter, concealment, funds, and any other assistance Rasul will need for his mission. Once completed, he will return to the masque until it is safe for him to leave the country. Marham's name means "smiling wish", which is appropriate because he will make all of us smile, and fulfill our wishes, when we strengthen our position in London and when we kill our nemesis Harold Gatewood."

Al-Din then asked for a vote on the mission of continued harassment and terrorist acts against London, and the killing of Harold Gatewood. The result was unanimous in favor of the mission.

Al-Din then called Rasul with the good news. "It is approved Halim. Do you have any questions?"

"Do you know when Gatewood will arrive?"

"No, but it will be soon, probably within a week."

"When do you expect the rebellions to begin in Ireland, Scotland, and Wales?"

"Soon. Or moles have told us that the CIO is sending Gatewood to those locations first, then to London to speak with the English Prime Minister."

"I will wait to kill Gatewood until he gets to our turf in London. We have the support from the masque and our believers in our area of London. Even the London police and the British military are afraid to come into our area."

"I told the committee that you will choose two believers to assist you in the operation. Is that enough?"

"Yes, I do not want to use a larger force because it would cause the police to monitor our movements. My two helpers are true believers and do whatever is needed to accomplish the mission."

"Very good Halim. Stay in touch and keep me posted on the mission."

"I will. In a few weeks we will have seized more control of London, and Harold Gatewood will be dead."

Chapter 15

OWFA

January 10

ALDOFITO IMANOL BOLTED UP THE STAIRS TO THE OWFA meeting room. Despite his age, being in the mid-fifties, he was on a mission today, and took the stairs two at a time so that he would be able to quickly enter the office and organize his notes for the important tasks at hand. He was optimistic about the news he had heard from Loretta Walters, his mole in the CIO.

Once he had arrived in his office, Imanol had taken time to consider how he would introduce the news to the committee. He would present his important message about how the organization should try to take advantage of the upcoming armed rebellions for total freed in Ireland, Scotland, and Wales.

He watched as each member entered the outer office and entered discussions with the other members already present. When all members had arrived, he walked to the meeting room, followed by the other OWFA committee office holders.

Imanol surveyed each member, sizing up their personalities, egos, loyalty to the movement, and personal makeups. He had accumulated damming personal files on each member, in case he would ever have to use the information as a political lever to swing a vote in his agenda's direction. Imanol loved the power he held over each member, and never hesitated to use it.

He looked at the twenty-five men who sat around the long, rectangular table, each sporting a concerned look on their face. The blue, green, and gold flag of their organization was on the wall on the right side of the room. Their organizational name, in the abbreviated capital letters OWFA, was housed in a ten-foot long by six-foot high glass case. The letters represented the organizational name, "One World For All".

Aldofito Imanol called the meeting to order and asked for the reports from each of the twenty-five regional commanders. After the reports were delivered, the OWFA commander, Imanol, an Argentinian multi-billionaire who was the main funder of the organization, spoke. "Comrades, we are here tonight to discuss an upcoming opportunity we will have in the near future that will help propel our mission for a one- world-government.

Our mole in the CIO has told me that Ireland, Scotland, and Wales will soon try to break from the British Empire, and demand independence. We know that these countries do not have the resources or the economic backing to make it on their own once they gain independence.

I am urging us to remain ready to usher these countries into our stable once they hit bottom. We will handpick the politicians that support our one-world view and make sure they are elected when the time is right. I am urging the committee to make the necessary planning arrangements and expenditures to be prepared for the moment we need them."

A vote was taken, and the measure was passed. Imanol then said that he wanted to mention the fine work that operative Gianna Sabina had done in Rome. After completing his review of Gianna's work he asked the committee for authorization to use her again if a future mission required her abilities. The committee unanimously approved the request.

Imanol then said, "In Rome, Harold Gatewood, a man who has foiled several of our missions and killed more than one of our agents, became enamored with Ms. Sabina. Adrianna's feelings were mutual and the two were intimate.

I believe that we can use her again when Gatewood goes to the British Isles to try to stop the independence movements of the three countries we discussed before. His actions would be in opposition to our goals. I will call her and discuss that possibility."

Imanol then said, "Long Live The OWFA!"

Chapter 16

"I miss him"

January 11

GIANNA SABINA HAD NOT SLEPT WELL SINCE SHE had left Rome. She had lost eight pounds off of her perfectly-shaped body, had developed large, dark circles under her eyes, and had cried for hours each day.

She had not been in love for years, and when she had met Gatewood she had fallen hard, loving him more and more each day. Her required sudden departure, and having to leave him unconscious and laying on the floor of the catacombs in Rome, had caused her much sadness.

She wanted to call him and explain why she had left, but she knew the OWFA would find out, and either terminate her employments, or worse, her life. She was unhappy, and did not want to speak with anyone.

Her cell phone rang, and begrudgingly, she answered.

"Gianna, this is Aldofito Imanol. How are you?"

She spoke a barely audible "Okay" and then remained silent.

"You don't sound well Gianna. What is wrong?"

"I have a bad cold."

"You need to get well soon because I have a mission for you. You will be going to the British Isles. Harold Gatewood will be there, and you can help us terminate him."

She perked up at the idea that she would be able to see Harold again, but she would never kill him, a fact that she would never mention to Imanol.

"Are you there Adrianna?"

"Yes."

"Are you interested in the assignment?"

"Yes."

"Excellent. I will be calling you with the details as soon as I hear back from our informant at the CIO."

"Fine. I will await your call Aldofito."

"Great. We are counting on you."

"I will not disappoint you Sir."

After clicking off her phone, she walked to the bathroom, splashed cold water on her face, dried off, and looked in the mirror. "I look awful. Harold would not even give me a second look unless I straighten myself out. I need to get ready in case I am called on to go to the British Isles. I have missed him. I love him, and I want to look my best. But, I will not kill him. Hopefully, I can go back to America with him when he leaves the British Isles."

Chapter 17

North Male Atoll, Maldives

January 13

IAN O'DONNELL WAS AN IRISH BUSIINESSMAN WHO had made his fortune in the laser optics industry. His systems were applicable to missile systems used in advanced weaponry by the American military. He was mega-rich, having hit it big in his early thirties. He had patented four generations of his systems, each one more-profitable, and more-desired by the members of the nuclear-club nations of the world.

He was a man who had stepped on his ex-partner, forcing him out of the business and taking complete control of the client accounts. The hatred between his ex-partner and himself was so thick it could not be cut with a machete. Each one wanted the other one dead.

His ex-partner had contacted a world-class contract killer to settle the score with O'Donnell. He had instructed the killer to make it quick, and deadly, as he wanted to end the feud as quickly as possible.

O'Donnell was a finance whiz and ran his company efficiently, which freed up time for him to enjoy his one true passion in life, surfing. He had traveled the world, riding the waves and searching for the world's best surfing thrills. He had hit nine of the top ten locations to "catch the perfect wave".

His favorite spot was the Banzai Pipeline in Oahu, Hawaii. He had also enjoyed the pleasures of the Mexican Pipeline's huge waves and great beach at Puerto Excon Dido in Oaxaco, Mexico, the pebble beaches, gray water, and long-range waves of Lima Peru, and the constant, tough, bug, tube waves of Jeffrey's Bay in South Africa.

In his quest to surf the top ten spots in the world, he had next gone to the Gold Coast of Australia, Zuma Beach in Malibu, California for its clean, but crowded beaches, and world-class breaks, and Manu Bay, Raglan, New Zealand for its quality surf, and exciting but dangerous barrel waves.

He had also mastered the surfing capital of Europe's dangerous waves at Hosse Gor, France, and the high waves and strong winds and beautiful beaches at Fuert Event-Ura, in the Canary Islands. Today, he was at North Male Atoll in the Maldives to finish out the top ten.

Today's location featured the longest waves and rides over one hundred yards anywhere in the world. Beautiful breaks and beaches combined to make this spot O'Donnell's favorite. He had checked out the area thoroughly before booking his trip. Peak time for the highest waves was between March and October but he was committed work-wise during all of those months.

He had his choice of surfing at any of the great areas at North Male, and had passed on the breaks at Chicken's, Coke's, Jailbreak, Sultan's, Ninja's, and Conch's points. He would surf the last of the top ten spots at Turtle Point, as it was the furthest point from the airport, was located on an uninhabited island, had eight foot waves at high tide, and was least impacted by the wind. It was his personal surfing heaven.

He was decked out in traditional surfing attire as he carried his board to the edge of the water, walked out to where the sea hit his waist, then hopped on his board and paddled out to the breaks where the biggest waves would start, and then carry him, standing upright on his board, all the way to within ten yards of the beautiful sand beach.

He had made three trial runs, falling on one and taking a beating by the waves that pounded him to the bottom after he had been tossed from his board. He waited in the water, lying flat on his stomach on his surf board, then paddled out to the breakers when the wind changed direction to blow from West to North.

One a hill above the beach on the deserted island, a contract-killer had assembled a weapon, being sure to attach the scope, an adjusting for wind direction by making two clicks. The killer then laid down on a blanket, and sighted in on O'Donnell while he paddled to the breaker.

The shooter suddenly felt queasy and rolled over on the right side of the prone body. Without warning, breakfast came flying out of the killer's mouth, landing on the soft green grass to the right. A second spewing of the last particles of the shooter's morning meal was then tossed to the right. Still feeling tipsy, the shooter felt droll fall from a mouth to the ground.

The shooter tried to stabilize the weapon and sight in O'Donnell who was just standing up on his surf board. Despite a struggle, and another urgent need to throw up, the shooter sighted in the surfer, placed the crosshairs of the scope on his heart and gently squeezed the trigger. The 30.06 round blasted through O'Donnell's heart, and he fell into the ocean, bleeding from his chest.

He had been dead before he hit the water, and once there the huge wave swallowed he and his surf board, and carried them on the wild ride that the

North Male Atoll was noted for delivering to those who dared surf one of the top sites in the world.

O'Donnell's body then floated face down in the water twenty yards offshore. With each incoming and outgoing wave, the corpse was carried out toward the breakers. The shooter had seen the killing shot hit the target, but then had once again pitched breakfast.

The shooter, alone on the island, then laid down and rested, going to sleep after five minutes, and awaking ten minutes later. Finally able to stand, the shooter's weapon was then broken down, placed in a case, and carried down the hill to a rental car, where weapon and shooter made their way toward the airport, their job completed.

Once on the plane back home, the shooter, Susana Richards, closed her eyes and thought, "Morning sickness is not fun. I hope the rest of my pregnancy will go smoother than today. I am actually concerned about what might lie ahead of me. I hope the twins will do okay and that they will both be healthy babies. But, I will be happy when this part of the experience is over."

When the plane was airborne, Susana asked the flight attendant of something that would settle her stomach. The flight attendant asked, "Is this your first baby?"

"Actually, it will be my first two babies."

"Twins. Oh how nice. Can I ask if your husband is handsome?"

"Yes, he is very handsome."

"Then with your beauty, and his handsome looks, you both are going to have two beautiful babies. And, your morning sickness will pass after a few days. I am so happy for you both."

Susana said thank you, then closed her eyes and thought, "Yes, our lives will be complete when the babies arrive. It will be perfect. I love you so much Harold."

Chapter 18

To Ireland

January 14

THE SNOWSTORM OF TWO DAYS AGO HAD PASSED, the sky was clear, and Gatewood was perched in seat 3 A ready to fly to Dublin, Ireland, the first stop of his mission.

He closed his eyes and thought about his destination. Dublin was the capital of the country, and served as an anchor for the city's economy. The city was rich in history, with a National Gallery that featured Irish art, specifically the works of native Impressionist painter Jack Yeats. Other works included those of Rembrandt, Picasso, El Greco, and the Italian Renaissance works of the eighteenth century.

The National museum highlighted the archeology, history, and culture of the country. The country's struggle during the potato famine in the mid-nineteenth century and the history of the early during the terror attacks in the nineteen-twenty-one uprising by the IOFFI was also detailed in the museum. Trinity College and its famous library was also a stop on the tourist tour.

The city's atmosphere included quaint pubs, theaters, hurling events, soccer matches, the Gaelic Games, entertainment options, numerous food choices, beaches, and Irish identity festivals that furthered Irish pride for its one million plus population.

Gatewood would center in Dublin during his mission, and then travel to Dublin and wherever else in Ireland that events may take him. He would meet with IOFFI leader Shamus Conri tomorrow, but for now he wanted to relax.

As he rested the names and places he had studied for his mission flashed through his mind. The Oireachtas was the upper house, and the Dail was the lower house of the Parliament, the Prime Minister of the country was the Taoiseach. The Ducas was branch of government in charge of parks and gardens, and DART was the Dublin Area Rapid Transit train line.

The RTE was the Radio Telifis Eireann was the country's national broadcasting service, the Iarnrod Eireann was the national railroad,

He then thought of the somewhat confusing terms, dates, and who's who of both the paramilitary groups that had battled out the question of Ireland's fate, either to remain as a part of the British Empire, or become independent and free.

Loyalists, Republicans, the IRA, Gardas, the Irish Republic police, the Blacks and Tans of the Royal Irish Constabulary. the Ulster Defence Associaion, Ulster, the Ulster Unionist Party led by Edward Carson, the IRA, Republican, Fianna Fail, Fina Gael, the Irish National Liberation Association, Sinn Fein, the Anglo-Irish Treaty of 1921, Eire, the official name for Ireland, the Royal Ulster Constabulary, the Republic of Ireland, and B-specials, were all terms that haunted Gatewood's mind as he tried to rest.

Irritated by his inability to sleep, Gatewood opened his eyes and thought, "I would go to a shebeen, an Irish speakeasy, settle into a partitioned off drinking area called a snug, have some fish and chops called chippers, listen to the bagpipes, called the uillean pipes, and watch a leprechaun dance on a table than having all of these confusing terms run through my mind."

He thought about breaking his no drinking rule by ordering a Vanducci single-malt whisky, but opted for a glass of water instead. He thought about his mission until he landed. Once in Dublin, he picked up his rental car, headed to his hotel, and checked into room one hundred.

After a restful night's sleep, he ate his usual breakfast, passing on the The Fry, the calorie-laden national breakfast, then walked in the cold January air around the city. He returned, ate a light lunch, and relaxed until he walked to a nearby pub to meet IOFFI leader Shamus Conri, and the head of the military wing of the organization, Alastar Cowal.

Both men had joined the organization in their teens, and had progressed up the rungs of the leadership ladder, always remaining loyal to each other, and the IOFFI. They had battled the Loyalists and the entrenched British government over the IOFFI's long-desired goal of independence. They had engaged in violent terrorists acts against their foes, a fact which they proudly admitted.

Their goal for independence for Ireland had remained strong, and they were now ready to reinstitute past violent measures against the British government.

Gatewood shook hands with both men, and then sat down. Shamus Conri was a stereotypical-looking Irishman, sporting a head of bright red hair, a thin face adorned with brown freckles, was five-feet-six-inches-tall, weighed one-hundred-forty-five pounds, and was obviously suffering from Napoleonic

Short-man syndrome. He was combative from his first statement to Gatewood.

Alastar Cowal was the opposite of Conri in terms of body build and looks. He had dark-black hair and eyebrows, and full beard. dark-brown eyes, was tall at six-feet-five inches, and weighed two-hundred-thirty-five pounds. He was quiet, and let Conri do the talking.

Gatewood, at the risk of his life, had tied not to laugh when he met the two men, as they were obviously the "Mutt and Jeff" version of Irish terrorist leadership.

After pleasant conversation, and the ordering of two pints for Conri and Cowal and a water for Gatewood, Harold had started the conversation. Before he was able to get a full sentence out of his mouth, Conri interrupted him by saying, "Stop! I don't trust a man who doesn't drink." He then proceeded to order a pint for Harold.

When the drink arrived, Harold took two sips and then set the pint aside. "Are you comfortable now Shamus?"

"Yes, very. Please continue."

Gatewood laughed, and then said, "What can I do for you two fine uasals?"

Both men laughed at Harold's compliment spoken their native language, and then Conri said, "How about an unlimited supply of weaponry to enforce our independence from the English."

Gatewood replied that he had heard Conri's organization had already filled that order from their supplier, the Chechen government. Conri laughed and said, "No, we dealt with a much more attractive lady who filled our order."

Without changing his facial expression, Harold had learned what he was fishing for in his question to Conri. His lover, Yua Hayato had supplied the weaponry for the IOFFI, no doubt buying the supply from Mayor Gennaro's corrupt administration. He said to himself, "Dam, Yua, you can't do those things if we are to remain friends. I can't keep shielding you from trouble if you keep that up."

Harold then asked Conri, "Is there another way we can work with the English government and the IOFFI to prevent that from happening?"

"No. England left their association with the other countries of Europe to protect their national interests. Now we are going to do the same."

"Do you think that violence can be avoided?"

"No. England will not listen to reason. We have tried to tell them for decades that we are Irishmen, not Englishmen. We want independence, the same type as exists for England, who just told the other European countries that very same thing, and then acted in their own self-interests when they left the trade group."

Have you given thought how our new country will survive economically if you leave the British Empire?"

"Yes. It could be no worse than it is now, being under their wing and having to pay them tribute for being part of the empire."

"What if they send troops here? If you start a war you will be operating like the Russians did in Afghanistan, and be bogged down for years, dealing with an occupying force."

"America also knows about that, as your country did the same thing. We should have never stopped fighting years ago. We accepted crumbs of limited representation in the British system rather than fighting until the London and Buckingham Palace squealed to end the stalemate."

"The world is an impatient place now. Do Irishmen and women have the patience to handle a long conflict? The citizenry may not have the backbone for a protracted battle."

"Mr. Gatewood, you pose excellent questions, but what makes you think the conflict may be a long one? London is besieged by problems. They have even elected their first Muslim worshiping mayor. They are going downhill and can't, and won't, even fight on one front, let alone on multiple ones. They have their hands full now, and will cave when other problems break out."

"You may be right Shamus. But, I would not want to see your fellow Irishmen die in the process."

"The countrymen who fall will become even more dangerous as heroes for the cause."

"I admire your spirit, but doubt that everyone is as dedicated as you."

"Perhaps, but our motto, 'We ourselves' did not mean that we would remain a part of Great Brittan. It meant one Ireland, free and independent."

Gatewood had tested Conri and had learned that the IOFFI was resolute in its goal of freedom. He was out of talking points.

Conri then said, "Harold, look at the Irish flag on the wall above my head. The green in the flag represents the past hopes of the Southern part of Ireland that worshipped Catholicism, and the Orange part represents the Protestant-worshipping Northern six counties of the country. The flag will be gone soon as the all of Ireland is now united to escape being held under England's thumb."

The three men shook hands, agreed to meet again tomorrow for more conversation about the issue of Irish independence, and then headed their separate ways. Gatewood had learned that negotiations for resolving the issue had little hope, and that Yua Hayato was buying guns from Mayor Gennaro and sending them to Ireland.

It had been a good day's work, and he decided to take a walk to clear his mind. He walked down one street, then the next, window shopping. He stopped in a small, quaint restaurant an ordered the "chippes" he had dreamed about on the airplane.

He noticed a beautiful, scarlet-red-haired lady enter the restaurant, head to a table, and sit down. As she took off her coat, she looked at him and smiled. She had bright blue eyes, was tall at five-feet-seven-inches in height, weighed around one-hundred-fifteen-pounds, was magnificently built, and looked as if she would to wear a size 2 dress.

After finishing his meal, Harold received his bull, proceeded to pay, and then left. He stopped at the second store on his way back to his hotel, a travel agency, and looked at the posters of a far-away beach location in the Turks and Caicos, a British Territory in the Bahamas. He found it ironic, based on his conversation with Conri and Cowal.

He laughed and then heard a voice behind him. "I think that is funny also, as not many people want anything to do with anything British these days."

Gatewood turned around and saw the beautiful red- headed woman from the restaurant. Surprised, he managed to stammer out an answer. After a few minutes of conversation he introduced himself. She followed suit, and said she was Nainsi Bebinn, an Australian woman who had returned to Ireland to visit her family, and to enjoy the sights of Dublin.

They talked and then decided to walk to the hotel where they were both staying. The conversation was easy and free-flowing, and they were soon in the hotel lobby. Harold asked her to join him for a drink, to which she agreed.

They continued their conversation until eleven-thirty, and then, after agreeing to take another sightseeing excursion the next day, said goodnight. He smiled at her as she entered the elevator, watching her face until the door closed, then walked to his room. She was very enchanting, and he was looking forward to being with her tomorrow.

After Nainsi Beninn returned to her room, her cell phone rang. "Yes, Shamus, we met, and things progressed nicely. He is very open with his conversation, and I believe I will find out exactly what he knows and what he is telling the CIO. I will keep you posted."

Harold met with Conri and Cowal four more times over the next six days, learning that the Carmelo and Masas Cartels, and the Fabbri Durante mafia family were supplying drugs to Conri's IOFFI, who were selling it in all of Ireland to finance their quest for weaponry and independence.

After Nainsi Beninn returned to her room, her cell phone rang.

He also learned that the TCPLM was helping ship massive amounts of drugs to Durante mafia in Italy, who then was delivering it to Conri. He had also caught wind of the fact that Venezuelan President Natalio Vicent had promised to furnish fighters if England moved military forces to Ireland.

Gatewood's mission was paying big dividends in terms of information, and Rick Owens was overjoyed with the news. When Harold was not speaking with Conri and Cowal he was spending time with Nainsi, hiking, eating, taking in a play, and enjoying each other's company.

They had become lovers on two days after their meeting in front of the travel agency, and were becoming close. When Rick Owens had asked Harold how much longer he needed to be in Ireland he had said, "Ten days" so he could spend more time with Nainsi.

After a scouting trip to Belfast to check out a lead about a drug delivery to the IOFFI from the Durante mafia, Harold returned to Dublin. Then, after seventeen days in Ireland, Gatewood kissed Nainsi goodbye, headed to the airport, and flew to Edinburg, Scotland for another round of information gathering.

Chapter 19

On To Scotland

January 31

UPON ARRIVAL, GATEWOOD PERFORMED THE usual duties at the baggage claim, and rental car agencies, and then headed to his hotel. After checking in to room one hundred, he reviewed his notes for his meeting with Conall Blair, head of the SPFIF.

Gatewood slept soundly, worked out, showered, and took a walk around Edinburg, the capital city of the country. The city on the hill had medieval history, beautiful gardens, and an array of spectacular neoclassical architecture.

After walking to Holyrood Park and climbing to Arthur's Peak, Harold scanned the city, taking in the layout of the historic city that had played such a big part in the country's development. He then headed to Edinburg Castle to see the crown jewels of the county and the Stone of destiny that was used in the coronation of Scotland's past kings, and ended up at Calton Hull to view the monuments of past heroes.

After playing tourist for the day, he returned to his hotel, relaxed, then walked to his meeting with Conall Blair. After reaching Blair's home, he was ushered into a sitting room to wait for his host. Gatewood had several reasons for meeting Blair. He wanted to assess Blair's commitment to leaving Great Britain's grasp, and find out if Scotland was also importing drugs from the cartels, guns from Yua Hayato, and had been promised fighting forces from Venezuela if England sent fighting troops to the area. He also hope to gather any new information that might be of help to his mission.

Blair appeared in the sitting room and asked Harold to join him in his office. The men shook hands, exchanged small talk, and then addressed the issues at hand. Blair was a man of average height and weight, at five-feet-ten inches and one hundred seventy pounds. He was not handsome or grotesque, strong or weak, powerful or meek, engaging or withdrawn, or nice or evil.

He was vanilla, without defining characteristics. He had only been passionate about one thing in his life, welsh independence from England. He had been the face of the SPFIF for many years, and had been a constant force who had recommended violence to gain independence.

During their conversation, Harold had noticed a note laying on Blair's desk, and had sneaked a peak when Blair had stood up to fill his pipe with tobacco from his stash on the counter behind him. It read, February 1, 8:30 P.M., dock 17, cargo containers 379 and 380, shipped from Chicago, Illinois.

After committing the note to memory, Gatewood again spoke with Blair, covering the same topics that he had addressed with Sham Conri in Dublin, Ireland. The rest of the conversation was as vanilla as Blair himself. The meeting had been pleasant, yet boring, but might have yielded significant importance related to message about the shipments coming into town tomorrow, the first of February.

After agreeing to meet with Blair in two days, Harold headed back to his hotel to have supper, without haggis, and then enjoy a good night's sleep.

The next day was spent working out, reporting to Rick Owens about the news concerning the shipments arriving from Chicago, Illinois later in the evening, and looking for clues that might signal where any drug shipments from Italy might be delivered. Gatewood guessed that the drop locations would be in the Scottish Highlands, due to its sparely populated areas.

At seven-thirty in the evening, Harold drove to the docks, and waited until eight p.m. in his car, then walked to dock 17, and waited. His wait was a short one as Conall Blair, the "Strong Wolf of the Battlefield", appeared, and waited by containers 379 and 380.

He was joined by an unidentified man who opened container 379, and the popped the lid of one of the many boxes inside, and took out a pistol, then a rifle. Blair inspected the weapons, smiled, shook hands with the man who had opened the container, and then left.

Three trucks then appeared, pulled up to the containers, loaded the boxes of weapons into the back of the vehicles, and then left, one after another, in military convoy fashion. Gatewood smiled, then said, "Compliments of Chicago Mayor Riccardo Gennaro, and the beautiful Yua Hyato, my lover, of Tokyo, Japan."

Gatewood then slipped away, unnoticed, and drove back to his hotel. He thought, "Gun running. This is getting more dangerous by the minute. I am happy this is my last mission."

The next day, Harold met with Blair once again, who was as vanilla as he had been two days ago. He gave Harold no clue that he had taken possession of a stash of weaponry to be used in the armed conflict with England for Scottish Independence.

When Blair again turned his back to repack his pipe with tobacco, Harold glanced at his appointment book.

Another notation was made for the next evening, 8:30 P. M., dock 17, containers 691 and 692, shipped from Chicago, Illinois.

The next evening, at precisely 8:30 P. M., Harold watched as the scene repeated itself. When the last of the three military-style trucks left with additional weaponry headed to the SPFIF.

Harold again reported the news to Owens, and then spent the balance of his week's stay in Scotland looking for clues to drug shipments from Italy into the country. No useful news about the drug shipments was found. Harold had come up dry in his attempts to tie Fabbri Durante to the drug smuggling operation. He might as well have spent his time looking for the Loch Ness Monster.

On the seventh of February, he would head to Wales.

Chapter 20

On To Wales

February 7

WALES WAS HAROLD"S LAST STOP ON HIS TOUR of the areas of the British Empire before his mission location switched to England. Gatewood had uncovered very useful information in Ireland and Scotland, and hope to do the same in Wales.

The country was located to the West of Liverpool, England, faced the Irish Sea on the North, Caernafon Bay and Cardigan Bay on the far West side of the country, and laid to the west of Bath, England, across the Severn River in the Southeast. .

The Northern area of Wales was mountainous, sparsely populated, and rural. The landscape was dotted with seventeen beautiful castles that had served as defensive strongholds, as they used round towers to watch for attackers, and faced the sea to spot any attack from the water.

The Western coastal town of Caernafon was famous for its slate mines that developed the best tops for pool tables in the world, scenic, and beautiful. On the Northern coast the cities of Conway and Bangor were quiet, peaceful, and quaintly unique.

The capital of the country was Cardiff, a city famous for its shipments of coal to the mother country by using the Severn River and the British Channel to the South. The city was famous for its castle, an opera house, and the capital buildings, where Wales had tried to gain autonomy and independence from England for many years. Cardiff would be Gatewood's home for his visit to Wales.

After arriving at his hotel, Gatewood smiled at the attractive young lady would assign him a room. Harold had smiled and then said, "Os gwelwch ya dda", which meant "please", when the woman had asked if he wanted room one hundred. He had then said, "Diolch", which meant "thank you", when the task was done.

He then headed to his room, checked the phone, the walls, and furniture for listening devices, and then relaxed until supper time. After supper, and a brisk walk, he returned, studied his material for the next morning's meeting with Einion Cryfder, the leader of the WISAM, and the man who would throw the switch to turn on the organization's use of violence against England.

The first meeting between Gatewood and Cryfder was less than pleasant. Cryfder kept Gatewood waiting for thirty minutes before allowing him to enter his office, and then was distant, bordering on rude, when Harold had asked him the same questions he had asked the independence movement leaders in Ireland and Scotland.

Cryfder was evasive and did not provide any details about the country's attitude toward violence against England. Gatewood realized that if the WISAM had plans to leave the British Empire in a violent manner, Cryfder was not going to tell them to him.

When Harold asked for a second meeting to try to address the issues that had been ignored, he was told that further discussion was "not necessary, as it was a matter to be handled by wales and the WISAM." He was then escorted from Cryfder's office, without the customary "thanks for stopping by" departing comment.

The trip had been a total bust. He called Rick Owens and asked how he should proceed in Wales. Owens; message was to "stick around one more day. If you can't find out any promising lead, or any useful information, leave the following day."

The next day continued the trend, and Gatewood's efforts were fruitless in terms of finding anything important. He then prepared to fly to his next stop, England.

Chapter 21

Boom

February 10

AFTER WORKING OUT AND EATING, GATEWOOD slept soundly until morning. He showered, and then turned on the television set. While brushing his teeth, he heard the report. A series of bombs had been exploded in the British Isles.

In Dublin, Ireland, a town which had suffered many terrorist attacks in the past, a car bomb had exploded near the main police station sending explosives into two patrolmen who stood on duty outside the building. One man was killed, and the second was in the hospital, in critical condition, and not expected to live.

A second explosion had destroyed much of the Grand Opera House in Belfast, the center of past IOFFI attacks from the start of the conflict with the English. The bombing had been a statement, and a reminder of past "war" with England, Three employees were hurt, and had been taken to the hospital.

IOFFI leader Shamus Conri had stated that the organization was responsible for the blast, and had then issued a demand to the English government for immediate independence. He had said that "this is just the beginning" if England did not grant independence before sunrise.

Rather than disparage the IOFFI, the media voiced support for the act and the demand for independence and had said that Ireland's independence was "long overdue."

Gatewood sat down on the bed, and thought, "I knew it. But, I did not think it would happen so quickly."

The television newscast then switched to Scotland, where two car bomb explosions had rocked the country. On the West coast, in Glasgow, a car bomb exploded near a restaurant where police personnel ate breakfast each morning. One officer had died, and seven were injured at the explosion's blast had shattered the front glass window of the restaurant, and sent explosive material into the faces and bodies of the police officer while they were eating.

In Edinburg, a car bomb had killed a member of the English Advisory Unit, the real power that ran the government. The explosive device was detonated when the car pulled up in front of the EAU's office, killing the driver and the head of the unit, and splattering explosive materials on other employees were entering the government building. One other employee was killed, and six more were injured in the explosion.

Conall Blair, head of the SPFIF, claimed responsibility for the incident, and issued a statement saying that "additional attacks will continue until England declares Scotland independent, and free from any ties to the English government."

In Wales, a Cardiff post office had been bombed, killing two federal workers, Englishmen who had been given their jobs after many Welsh citizens had been passed over and not given the opportunity to work. Seven other employees, all English men and women were injured and now in the hospital.

Einion Cryfder, head of the WISAM, had immediately claimed the organization's responsibility for the blast, and had issued a warning, that "all Englishmen would be driven from Wales, never to return, and that soon, wales would be independent, and the British flag would be burned on the steps of the capital building."

Gatewood sat in silence as the news report continued. Six people, all English, had been killed, and seventeen others, all English, had been injured and hospitalized. He had been right when he had told Owens that "violence would soon break out."

The bad news continued as a special report on television discussed a breaking story that "incidents of terror had broken out in London, Liverpool, and Bath."

A bomb had exploded in London, killing twelve citizens and one American as they walked to work in the financial district. Another twenty-three had been injured in the blast, as shrapnel from the bomb had flown in man directions, sending jagged pieces of steel and ball bearings into the crowd.

In Liverpool, a blast had killed a police officer when he stopped to visit with a citizen on the street. The citizen has injured, hospitalized, and in critical condition, not expected to survive.

In Bath, five citizens had been killed when a bomb was detonated in front of a government office building, as the reported to work. Three more citizens were injured and listed in varying physical conditions in the hospital.

The USFF had immediately claimed responsibility for the carnage in all three locations, saying that "England will soon be ruled by those who worship Allah. Our jihad will continue until we are in total control."

Gatewood tallied up the toll caused by the USFF in England. Nineteen people had been killed, including eighteen English citizens and one American. Twenty-seven English citizens had been injured and hospitalized.

Harold then totaled up the deaths and injured in all of the attacks on the British Isles. Twenty-six people had been killed and fifty-four people had been injured and hospitalized. The IOFFI, SPFIF, WISAM, and the USFF all had claimed their responsibility for the incidents, and had vowed that today's horrors were just the start of what promised to be a series of bloody terrorist wars on British soil.

Gatewood called Owens who told him to sit tight and see what happened in the next few hours. Then they would decide where Gatewood would go, and who he would speak with concerning the terrible situations. Harold clicked off his cell phone and tried to think about his actions during his mission. He wondered if he had missed any clues that would have alerted him to the fact that the attacks were on the verge of breaking out.

After much thought, he said, "I did all that I could, and I did not miss anything. I reported my findings to Owens, and waited for instructions. I have done everything a person could have done. I was right about one thing, the British Isles were about to be set on fire."

Chapter 22

To London

February 12

GATEWOOD HAD THOUGHT ABOUT THE TERRORIST attacks of the tenth, and had not come up with a thread that would have signaled the multiple events occurrence. They were years in the making, and had given no cue of when they would have happened.

On his flight to London, he thought about the once great British Empire that now appeared to be weak, and crumbling from attacks from inside and outside of its boundaries. The empire consisted of the country, colonies, protectorates, and territories overseen by the United Kingdom.

The fifteenth and sixteenth centuries had seen the accumulation of overseas possessions and trading posts that had led to the building of the largest empire in the world. For over one hundred years, the British Empire was a global power that ruled over four hundred million people, almost a quarter of the world's population, and an area that was equal to one-fourth of the world's geographic area.

The slogan that "The sun never set on the British Empire" was true, as the British were the political, legal, and cultural leaders of the world. Soon, hey were challenged by Spain and Portugal for the acquisition of new colonies and trade routes. In the seventeenth and eighteenth centuries, new competition France and Netherlands teamed up to challenge the English and Scottish claim as the number one power in the world.

The British expanded in the Indian continent through the trade obtained by their East India Company and through wars. America split off from England in seventeen-hundred-seventy-six, but the British went after new territory in Asia, Africa, and in the Pacific Ocean.

After wars with France, Britain built itself into the number one military power in the world, and became the policeman for the world. The Industrial Revolution of the nineteenth century enhanced the empires strength, which allowed them to expand into India and deeper into Africa. Control of those colonies enhanced the empire's trade and they continued to expand economically.

In England, free trade continued to be beneficial until the increase and urbanization of the population led to social and economic downturns for the country. The need for new markets, and new supplies of raw materials to turn into tradeable goods fueled more overseas colonization, and the expansion into Egypt.

New challenges from Germany and the United States led to a weakening of the empire, as did World War I and II. Prior to World War II, the empire shrank as Japan took over the empire's colonies in Southeast Asia, and India and other colonies were granted independence. The proverbial end of the empire took place when England returned Hong King to China.

Gatewood shook his head after thinking about how the once-great British Empire had gone downhill over the years. Now, it had fourteen territories it controlled.

Akortiri and Dhekella in Cyprus, Anguilla, Bermuda, the British Virgin Islands, the Cayman Islands, the Turks and Caicos, the Falkland Islands, Gibralter, Montserrat, and territories in the Atlantic, Indian, and Pacific Oceans were all that were left of the empire.

Gatewood wondered how an empire could fall so far. As a boy he had studied the great kings and queens of England who had built the empire and the country. First monarchs on the list were William I, aka William the Conqueror who fought the Norman Conquest, King Alfred who united the country and defeated the Viking invaders, and Queen Victoria who reigned the longest of any monarch had increased the size of the empire and ushered in the Industrial Revolution.

Their successes augmented by those of Richard I, aka Richard the Lionhearted, who had fought in the crusades, Henry V, who unified the country and provided stability, and Queen Elizabeth I, who stabilized the country after the turmoil of Henty VIII.

Other great monarch who had forged the empire's success included King Edward I, who developed the governmental and the legal systems of the country, King Edward VIII, who developed social and economic gains, and King Arthur and his famed Knights of the Roundtable.

England and the empire had vaulted heroes whose names had survived history and helped build the empire to its greatness. Robin Hood of Sherwood Forest fame, Sir Walter Raleigh, who was an explorer who sailed to find the North American continent, Oliver Cromwell, who developed the domestic government, Sir Francis Drake, who explored the world and defeated the Spanish armada, Benjamin Disraeli, who was the most important statesman for Queen Victoria, were all heroes.

Winston Churchill, the one man Adolf Hitler of Germany knew could stop his defeat of Europe and his march to world domination, Margret Thatcher, the "Iron Lady" who was the first woman Prime Minister of England, Charles Darwin, the man who developed the theory of natural selection and evolution, and William Shakespeare, the great author were also heroes.

Sir Isaac Newton, who developed the law of gravity, Sir William Wallace of Scotland, Sir Charles Chaplin of comedic and movie fame, Stephen Hawking, the astrophysicist who developed the theory of quantum gravity, poet Geoffrey Chaucer, and author Charles Dickens, and John Lennon and The Beatles were also heroes who had given the empire its glorious historical past and significance.

Gatewood shook his head and said, "I wonder what all of the great British Empire heroes and figures would say today, after the terrible terror attacks of the tenth. I am sure they would be disappointed with not only those events, but with the hordes of illegal immigrants that England, and specifically London, have taken in at the expense of their culture and history. I am certain that all of them would be very disgusted and disappointed."

Gatewood's thoughts then turned to his mission. He was scheduled to meet with the English Prime Minister, Kendrick Haven, Head of National Security Baldwin Dana, and the first London Mayor who worshiped Islam, Ihab Nima, on successive days.

Originally, their discussions were to address the potential movement for independence in Ireland, Scotland, and Wales, on terrorism in general, and how America could help stop the illegal immigration flow into England that was crippling the country. Now, since the balloon had popped, and terror attacks and the calls for independence had broken out in Ireland, Scotland, and Wales, the topics to be discussed would be different, and more complicated.

Gatewood shook his head and again said, "I am certain that all of the noted heroes of the British Empire would be very disgusted and disappointed with the current state of affairs."

In Argentina, OWFA leader Aldofito Imanol spoke into his cell phone, "Yes, that is very useful information. We will deposit your usual fee into your overseas account. We are always very thankful for your excellent work, and we look forward to working with you again."

Imanol then smiled, and thought for a moment. He then said, this may be the best fifty thousand dollars we have ever spent."

He then dialed a number and spoke, "Hello Gianna. I have news for you. Gatewood is flying to London today. He will be there for a few days. I want you to go to London on the next flight. Find Gatewood, follow him, find out what he is accomplishing in London, and report back to me. After we have learned all we need to know, you are ordered to kill him."

Gianna Sabina meekly said yes to the mission, clicked off her phone, and thought. "I took the mission so no one else would have it, as they would kill Harold. I will not. I will find him, and convince him to take me to the American Embassy in London. He can then help me get to the United States. I am going to tell him that I love him, and that I want to be with him the rest of my life."

Chapter 23

The Prime Minister

February 13

BRITISH PRIME MINISTER WAS IN HIS OFFICE AT five-thirty in the morning on the thirteenth. His eyes were home to bags that had accumulated due to having only one hour's sleep. He sipped a cup of tea with lemon, and looked at the overnight reports that were stacked on his desk.

He sighed and said, "It has come to pass. All three of them, the IOFFI, the SPFIF, and the WISAM, have declared war on the British Empire. I knew this might happen but I am shocked that it happened so quickly. They were preparing for this action months before our intelligence told us, and they are many steps ahead of us."

The Prime Minister, the head of Her Majesty's Government in the United Kingdom, had been in office for only a little over a year. Yet, he had dealt with more problems than most of his predecessors had faced in their entire careers. The world had increasingly become a more-dangerous place even during his tenure in office.

He had gone to the best boarding schools in the country during his youth, enrolled in his father's alma matter, majored in finance and political science, and had won a Rhodes Scholarship to Oxford where he had received his DPhil, his Doctorate in Philosophy. He had always dreamed of going to Oxford, as its history as a world-renown university had started shortly after the Norman Conquest in 1066.

He had sharpened his research skills at Oxford, and used that ability to full advantage when he entered the British Navy for a stint in the Intelligence Corps. After his military career he had entered the world of banking, rising to a high-level position with one of the better banks in the country.

He was convinced to enter politics and had moved up the rungs of the conservative party, serving as a member of the Parliament, the Foreign Secretary, and then the First Lord of the Treasury. He had won the recent election over the liberal Labour Party candidate who had refused to refute the policy of accepting the waves of illegal immigrants who had made their way through Europe to London.

He, Kendrick Haven, had won the election in a landslide, as the English citizenry wanted to reverse the elimination of their heritage and culture by the illegal immigrants who refused to work, lived off the dole, and had completely changed the population makeup of London, which was now called Londinistan.

Haven was tall at six-feet-four-inches, fit at one- hundred-eighty pounds, left-handed, had gray hair, wore glasses, married, had three daughters, loved to play tennis, was an avid pheasant hunter and fisherman, was well-liked by political party, and worked effectively with the opposition party.

His political skills would be tested over the remainder of his term, as the problems England faced could not be solved quickly, and they certainly weren't going to disappear on their own. He needed help, from any and all qualified sources.

Haven slugged his way through the reports, and the morning. It was almost noon when his secretary informed him that Harold Gatewood was waiting in the outer lobby for the luncheon meeting. He organized his papers, and placed them in four nice, neat piles on his desk, one each for Ireland, Scotland, wales, and London.

He said hello to Gatewood, and then the two walked to his personal dining room where they exchanged opening conversation until lunch arrived. Over the meal, they talked about the events that had broken out, and how the United States could be of help to England.

Haven asked Gatewood about what he had learned on his recent stops in the three colonies that had just exploded in terror acts related to their demands for independence. They then talked about the illegal immigrant population problems in London. Haven admitted that he was having trouble trying to convince London's mayor, Ihab Nima, that the masques in the city were the hotbed of the terrorist attacks.

Although he could not prove it, Haven's opinion was that Nima was being used by the masque and the USFF to purposely, or accidently, further the terror group's interests. Haven was handcuffed politically as he could not criticize Nima publicly for what he thought the mayor was doing in the name of Allah, and at the expense of England.

Haven wondered if Gatewood had any thoughts on the topic. Gatewood agreed to talk with the mayor, and then investigate any unusual incidents that might come up in their conversation.

The two men covered several topics, and were of like mind on what had to be done. The answer to how to do it was, unfortunately, not forthcoming during their meeting. Both men parted as friends, and Haven promised to help Gatewood in any way he could during his stay.

The meeting had lasted an hour and thirty minutes. While it was short in duration, it was long on frustration, as the roadmap to the needed actions was littered with political, and religious, landmines. Only time, trust, and expert political skills could lead Haven to the desired actions.

Gatewood headed to his hotel, changed into his workout clothes, and took the lift down to the lower level of the building where the workout facility was located. To his dismay, it was closed for remodeling. He took the lift up to the first floor, and asked the front desk clerk if there was anywhere else he could work out.

The desk clerk apologized for the inconvenience and gave Gatewood a pass for the workout facility across the street. After retrieving his coat, Gatewood walked across the street, presented his pass, and entered the facility. He did the same workout he had been doing for years, stretching, tai chi, taekwondo, Brazilian jiu-jitsu, light weights, and a brisk walk, this time on a treadmill.

Five minutes into his walk on the treadmill a beautiful woman smiled at him, and stepped on the treadmill next to him, and started to walk. Gatewood smile back, and thought, "I hope this is my lucky day." After five more minutes the beautiful woman said, "I saw you working out. You have a very unusual workout routine. How long have you been using it?"

"For many years. By the way I saw you working out also. You stay in great shape."

She said thank you and then continued to talk with Harold for twenty more minutes. Then she said, "I have had it." Gatewood answered, "Me too", and then asked her if she would like to get a glass of water or something else to drink.

She said "Yes. Let's go to the coffee shop in the hotel across the street."

They found a table and talked, finding out that they had much in common. After learning about each other
and finishing their water and tea with lemon, she said she had to go home.

"What is your name Mam?"

"Cindy Almas. What is yours?"

"Miss Cindy Almas, I am Harold Gatewood. He then took his business card from his pocket, handed it to her with the writing on the card facing her, as he had learned in Japan when he played for the Tokyo Cardinals, and the bowed his best bow, as he had also learned in Japan.

She smiled, giggled, and said thank you. He then asked her out to supper the next evening and she said yes. They exchanged cell phone numbers and then walked to the front door of the hotel. Gatewood opened the door for her, and took her left arm to help her down the steps. She said thank you, and that she would text him the address of the restaurant after she returned home. They smiled at each other, and said goodbye.

Gatewood showered, went to the hotel restaurant for supper, and then returned to his room. Within ten minutes a text came in on his phone. It listed the directions to the restaurant, and a note which read: I enjoyed meeting you today, and I am looking forward to our date tomorrow evening. I will see you them. Cindy.

Gatewood smiled, acknowledged her text by saying "You have a date Beautiful", and eventually fell asleep later that evening, after thinking about his upcoming evening with Cindy.

Chapter 24

The Head of National Security

February 14

NO TERROR ACTS HAD TAKEN PLACE IN THE three English states, or in London, since the tenth. It was as if everyone was waiting for the other parties to react before kicking in the next aggressive phase of the independence movements, and the advancement of the USFF agenda in London.

Gatewood arrived early for his meeting with Baldwin Dana, the Head of National Security for the country. When Harold entered Dana's office his first impression of the man was very positive. He was six feet tall, weighed two hundred pounds, had not one ounce of fat on his body, was affable, smiled easily, was widowed four years ago, had been the British Army, had spent his entire working career working as a policeman, and was a "no-nonsense, law-and-order-type of guy.

Danna was interested in the type of weaponry Gatewood had seen in Scotland, and if he had noticed any activity in Ireland, the home of past brutal, dangerous, terrorist activity. Despite not having much information for Dana, the National Security Director was happy because any lead was better than none.

Prior to the attack, Dana had been working with Prime Minister Haven on a new, updated security plan for the country. The plan addressed domestic and foreign terror attacks, the delivery of weapons and explosives via air, land, or sea routes. They had installed a more comprehensive tracking-system for cargo arriving by sea but no weaponry had turned up in England that might be headed to terrorists.

Dana was also interested in Gatewood's impressions of Shamus Conri and Alastar Cowal of the IOFFI, Conall Blair of the SPFIF, and Einion Cryfder of the WISAM. After comparing the British profile on each with Gatewood's perceptions of the men, possible new facts that might help in negotiations were uncovered.

Dana's security plan for the country was sound, and had impressed Gatewood with its detail, and list of action steps to take when a terror incident occurred. The meeting ended on positive terms and each man was totally committed to help each other if a terror incident broke out while Gatewood was in the country.

Gatewood headed back to his hotel, worked out, showered, and readied himself for his date with Cindy Almas. She was truly gorgeous. At five-feet-three-inches tall, one-hundred-five pounds in weight, possessing a perfect waist-to-hip ratio of .7, an hour-glassed figure, large breasts, long black hair that stopped in the middle of her back, beautiful dark-brown "bedroom eyes", a perfectly-shaped mouth filled with straight, white teeth, long, slender fingers, a proportionately-shaped nose, "olive-colored skin", and a devastating smile, she was just Gatewood's type.

Long ago, Susana Richards had ordered him to "be a good boy" when he was away from her. But, he was not married yet, and the gorgeous Cindy Almas might be his "going away present" from singlehood. No matter which way it might go, he knew that he would enjoy being with her in London while he kept a watchful eye on developments related to terror and demands for independence.

He looked at his cellphone to see the time. He had less than an hour to wait before he should leave to meet Cindy.

Chapter 25

A Knockout

February 14

GATEWOOD ARRIVED EARLY AT THE RESTAURANT and waited inside the door for Cindy to arrive. He saw her walk toward the door, so he opened it and took her right arm, and helped her enter the waiting room. She smiled and he returned the greeting, noticing that her eyes were dilating. They talked for fifteen minutes while they waited for their reserved table.

Throughout the evening they grew closer to each other, enjoying each other's company more with each passing moment. They were the last to leave, and after exiting the front door, stopped to talk. After a few minutes of talking, Harold said, "Which way?"

She kissed him passionately, and said, "Back to your room." They talked as they walked, holding hands and laughing. And soon they were at the hotel, in the lift from the lower main floor to the floor where his room was located. Once the door was opened they kissed their way to the bed, removed each other's clothes with in record time, and made passionate love until early morning.

Harold felt a soft kiss on his eyelids, then opened his eyes to see Cindy's face above him. She said, I watched you while you slept. I love to hear you talk, but you are also very enchanting when you are asleep."

He laughed and said thank you, then they talked for ten minutes, and once again then made love again. She needed to go to work at her job at the record store, and he was scheduled to meet with the mayor of London, Ihab Nima, for a late-morning meeting. They showered together, made plans to meet to work out and spend the evening together, kissed each other goodbye, and then headed in opposite directions.

At the record store, Cindy could not keep her mind on business matters, as she was thinking about Harold. As Harold waited in the waiting room of London's mayor, he could not concentrate on the topics to be discussed, as his mind was on Cindy.

After being escorted into Ihab Nima's office, the men shook hands, exchanged hellos, and talked about the mayor's duties related to terror and the safety of London.

Nima had been elected by a slim margin in the last election. All political sides of the city were angry. Those who did not follow the Islamic faith raged that the election was not fair, and said the votes from the Muslim communities were counted more than once to give victory to Nima, a loyal member of the masque led by Tabassum Marham, a reputed supporter of the USFF.

USFF.

The Muslin community and the militant –supporting masque had argued that Nima had been legally elected in the nine-candidate race, and that no illegal counting of the ballots had taken place. The full year of Nima's tenure had been marked with accusations, threats, and very questionable decisions on several matters, all of which had ended up supporting the masque's questionable actions.

Gatewood listened intently as Nima presented a disjoined, unusual plan of action to which he had committed London to follow. Gatewood was not a city planner, but it was obvious that certain parts and citizens of the city were benefiting more than others.

Harold empathized with Prime Minister Haven and National Security Head Dana, as they were fighting an uphill battle with Mayor Nima's plans for the city as they related to terror attacks and a sanctuary city policy to protect illegal immigrants.

London was at odds with the rest of the country. After concluding his meeting with the mayor, Gatewood thankfully escaped. As he walked to back to his hotel, he thought, "I actually feel like I am back in Chicago. Gennaro and Nima must be brothers. At the very least they are kindred spirits."

Chapter 26

Progress

February 28

AFTER HIS MEETING WITH MAYOR NIMA, HAROLD had called Rick Owens with his report on the Prime Minister, the national Security Director, and London's mayor. Owens advised Harold to stay in London, and continue to monitor the situation related to the troubles in Ireland, Scotland, and Wales, and to try to find out anything in London related to potential terror plans.

Harold and Cindy were getting along wonderfully, becoming closer, and spending most all of their days and nights together. They were enjoying their enthusiastic love-making sessions, and were always anxious to be with one another.

Harold had not understood two things about Cindy. One, she never mentioned her parents unless he asked about them. He had never met them, and did not understand how they could seem so unimportant to Cindy, as she did not harbor any resentment against them. Second, he had not figured out how a beautiful English girl like Cindy could have olive-colored skin, as most English women had fair complexions. He had asked her about it, and she had said that there was some "Spanish blood" on her father's side of the family.

Cindy usually spent two nights a week away from Gatewood, saying she needed to work evenings at the record store. The arrangement was fine with Harold, as he needed time to investigate certain matters that he uncovered when he scouted for information relevant to his mission during the day.

Little did Gatewood know that when he was out during the day a pair of eyes had been watching him every step of his way. His lack of knowledge might cause his death one day.

In the late afternoon, new terror attacks broke out in Belfast, Ireland, Edinburg, Scotland, and Cardiff, Wales. Bombs were exploded, policeman were shot by long-range snipers, and British troops who had been sent to the areas to prevent further violence had been mowed down by a hail of rounds from machine guns wielded by IOFFI terrorists in Belfast.

Twelve British military personnel were killed or injured, three British-installed civil service employees in Cardiff were blown to bits by a letter bomb, and four British troops were killed while on a reconnaissance mission on the outskirts of Edinburg.

In London, four British citizens and two American tourists were chopped to death by a Syrian member of the USFF who was wielding a machete near Big Ben.

Terrorism had revisited the British Isles in a big way, and none knew when the onslaught might end.

Prime Minister Kendrick Haven and National Security Head Baldwin Dana met to consider how to proceed in London, and the three states of the British Isles. Haven was in favor of sending in more British troops, but Dana advised him to send in more undercover operatives to monitor the movements of the leaders of the terrorist groups in Ireland, Scotland, and Wales. Dana convinced Haven that more visible British troops in the areas would only provide more targets for the terrorists.

Both Haven and Dana deployed more British troops to protect the areas where the tourists gathered to see the historic sites such as Big Ben, Buckingham Palace, the Tower of London, and Piccadilly Square. The move was fought vigorously by London Mayor Ihab Nima, but he eventually agreed to the decision, but registered his complaint that the move further divided the regular citizenry and the communities with heavy Muslin-worshiping populations.

Harold called Rick Owens, and was again advised to stay in London, as he had sent agent Jack Taylor to Belfast, Ireland to look for the sources of the attacks.

Gatewood was relaxing in his room when Cindy arrived from work. Despite being tired, she kissed him, led him to the shower, then to the bed, and made love with him for an hour. Afterwards, she asked if they could go out for supper. Harold suggested that they stay in the hotel and eat at the restaurant, as there had been too many terrorist attacks to venture out on the street. She obliged, and after the meal the couple relaxed in the room, made love, and before closing their eyes and entering sleep, they talked about the terror attacks.

Cindy had been riding the bus to work, an act which Gatewood considered dangerous. He suggested that she take a taxi every day, as the terrorists usually preferred to attack where many citizens were congregated. She thanked him for his concern about her safety, kissed him goodnight, an immediately fell asleep.

Harold looked at her while she slept, admiring everything about her. He ran his hand over her soft, olive-colored skin on her forearm, and wondered, "It still doesn't make sense. How can she have olive-colored skin if both of her parents are full-blooded English natives." He kissed her, pulled her close to him, wrapped his arms around her, and said, "It doesn't matter." He then closed his eyes and went to sleep.

Chapter 27

At The Masque

March 1

MUSLIM IMAN TABASSUM MARHAM attended to his duties at the masque, then walked to his private dining room, and after praying, prepared for a private meeting and lunch with USFF operative Halim Rasul, who had been staying in the masque to prevent being recognized as a terrorist on English soil in London.

The sanctuary provided by the masque had allowed Rasul to carry out his training of two other USFF terrorists, Abdel Nour and his sister, for the mission in London. Rasul told Marham that the two other USFF agents had been making nice progress in their training, and were almost ready for the mission.

The three agents had made a trial run, performing all of the acts of the mission except the actual detonation of the bomb that would kill up to one hundred fifty people, and create havoc that might lead to countless other deaths in London.

While Abdel Nour had been programed to become a martyr for the USFF cause, his sister was a concern for Rasul, as she did not seem to have the total commitment to the USFF's cause that her brother had accepted without reservation. The young woman seemed to be concerned with worldly matters, and Rasul was concerned that she might not follow through with her part of the mission. Her indecision might derail the mission.

He had decided to put her to a test to make sure she had the grit and determination to follow the plan that would advance the USFF's agenda. She had passed the test, but Rasul still sensed a hesitation in the young woman. He had asked Iman Tabsassum Marham to have Abdel and his sister's father come to the mission so he might have the opportunity to talk with him.

The elder Nour arrived, exchanged greetings, and then prayed. Rasul then spoke, "Mr. Nour, please be honest with me. Do you think that your daughter has the dedication to Allah to follow through on a mission that the USFF has mapped out here in London?"

"I do. She is not as outgoing or animated as her brother Abdel, bus she is a determined young lady who was taught to honor her commitments, especially to Islam. She can be counted on to perform as instructed."

"Have you noticed any change in your daughter?"

"Yes, she has been very happy in the last two-and- one-half weeks, the happiest I have ever seen here. Once in a while she goes the other way, being very despondent, feeling down and despondent. But, she bounces back very quickly."

"How many days a week does this occur?"

"Two days a week."

"Are the despondent periods following a set schedule?"

"Yes, like clockwork."

"What is different on those days?"

"She stays with us to see her mother and I."

"Where does she stay the other five nights?"

"At her apartment."

"Do you find that strange?"

"No, not really. I think she is just a self-reliant young woman, and staying with us breaks her lifestyle pattern."

"Have you talked with her about it?"

"Yes. She has said that it is a change that requires her to get up much earlier, as she has about twice as far a distance to get to work when she stays with us."

"Alright, I think she will be fine for the mission. If she is losing sleep and traveling much further to work, then that is probably the reason. Try to convince her to get more sleep when she stays with you and your wife. I thank you for coming to the masque to talk with me. You have been very helpful."

Rasul was satisfied that Abdel's sister was still an acceptable operative for the mission. He would have both of them ready in a few more days.

Chapter 28

From Damascus

March 6

A PHONE CALL CAME IN TO HALIM RASUL FROM Damascus. Ala Al-Din, leader of the USFF inner circle and the main council of the organization spoke to Rasul, "How is the mission progressing Halim?"

"I believe it is in good shape at this point. The two operatives have almost mastered the training required to successfully carry out the mission. Abdel Nour has shown great dedication to the cause, and has been a loyal soldier for Allah. I think he will go far in the organization. He is a rising star."

"What about his sister? Does she share his dedication?"

"She is struggling because she has one foot in our cause, and one foot in the modern world. She shows flashes of brilliance, but needs to make a full commitment to the USFF's purpose. She makes great progress then slides backwards. She comes from good, strong Islamic stock, and will be fine once she puts the modern world in the rear view mirror. She is a diamond in the rough."

"Will she be ready for the mission?"

"Yes, she is on the edge of a breakthrough. I invited her father to the masque recently to discuss how he can help us have her make a total commitment. He says that she has been staying with them two nights a week, which causes her to lose sleep and travel an extra distance to work. I think the father is concerned about her commitment, but was afraid to discuss it with me for fear of reprisal."

"Have you set the date for the mission?"

"I am almost ready to do that. I am going to have Abdel and his sister come to the masque, visit with Iman Tabassum Marham reaffirm with them how to live a life dedicated to Allah. I think that they will accept the mission whole heartedly."

"Halim, how are you doing? Are you comfortable with the mission?"

"Truthfully, I have been thinking about my own life. We have been with the USFF since we were boys. We have fought man battles for Allah, and have always been loyal soldiers. I want to ask you a question."

"Please do so Halim."

"Have you ever regretted the fact that you might have done something else with your life?"

"No, I am happy with my life. It has been a great honor to serve Allah. What is bothering you?"

"I am honored to serve the USFF also. But, I wonder how my life would be different if I had not joined the movement. I have no wife, no children, no family. I know I will go to see Allah when I die, but I have really enjoyed no personal joy in my life. It is if I have never been born, or made a mark on the world up to this point."

"You will make your mark in the world when you lead your two soldiers on the upcoming mission."

"I know. I do not mean to be blasphemous to Allah, but I had hoped for some personal joy in my life. If I am to make my mark with this mission, then I will do it. I will always be a good soldier for the cause. I do not mean to sound weak, but I wanted to speak with you about this so I could purge it from my mind. Please do not think less of me for bringing it up with you."

"I would never do that Halim. You will have your moment in the sun with this mission, an you will be rewarded in the afterlife. All of the members of the council have total faith in you. We could not have picked a better man to accomplish the upcoming task."

"Thank you. I will not fail."

After the conversation, Ala Al-Din clicked off his phone. Halim Rasul sat quietly, thinking about his boyhood when he was happy. He had loved his home country of Syria. He was a good student in the madrassas and learned the prayers and teachings of Islam's leaders.

He had then become interested in the USFF, and became an operative, who was willing to give up his life for the cause. Soon, he would perform that task again, and trust his life with two new operatives, one who had total dedication, and one whose hesitation might cost all of them their lives.

He had not told Abdel and his sister that the mission was much more dangerous than he had led them to believe. In fact, it could be classified as a suicide mission. He had wondered why he was chosen to lead the operation. It had finally dawned on him that he was replaceable, and a man no one would miss if he perished in the line of duty.

He had his fears, and this mission had brought them to the forefront of his mind. He had struggled with his mortality since he had arrived in London, and had convinced himself that if had to die, he would take many infidels with him. He had been ordered to also kill Harold Gatewood if he had the opportunity to do so. He would love to do just that if he was given the chance.

Tabassum Marham had walked into the room where Rasul stayed and where he had spoken to Ala Al-Din. Marham spoke, "I know what you are feeling Halim. I have felt that way myself until I realized my destiny was to serve the USFF and further the teaching of Mohammed. We are all just men, with human feelings, doubts, and fears. Give yourself to Allah and things will work out the way they have been destined to happen. It will be alright Halim."

"Thank you Tabassum."

Chapter 29

Ready, Set...

March 5

WHILE GATEWIID WAS EATING BREAKFAST IN HIS hotel room he received a call from CIO agent Jack Taylor. The two men, who had waged many battles together for the CIO, talked about what was happening in the British Isles.

Gatewood asked, what is happening out there in the countryside?"

"The terrorist bombs are in full bloom across Ireland, Scotland, and Wales. What his happening in Londinistan Harold?"

"There are bombs going off here also, plus machete-wielding zealots who are anxious to make their trip to see Allah."

Harold, I have used your reports to try to find out when more guns and explosives will arrive in each of the three countries. Yua Hayato and the Yakaza are making a fortune, as countless weapons and ammunition are flowing into the area."

"Don't forget her supplier, Mayor Gennaro of Chicago."

"Right. His signature is all over this situation also. Have you turned over anything in London?"

"Nothing recently. I know there is terrorist activity going on and that something big will probably take lace soon, but I haven't fund it yet. Today, I am going to stake out the masque that is the most pro-USFF in the city. It is run by the Iman Tabassum Marham. Maybe I can see something important."

"Are you having any fun, besides work, Harold?"

Gatewood laughed and said, "Of course."

"You have another beautiful roommate don't you Harold?"

Gatewood laughed and said, "Of course Jack, you know me too well."

"How beautiful is she /'

"Very. She is a wonderful, tender, loving, wonderful lady. I will hate to leave London."

After more conversation about their missions, Taylor told Gatewood to "Be careful", an then heard the same words come out of his fellow-agent's mouth.

Cindy had left for work at the record shop and would be staying with her parent tonight, which would give Gatewood an opportunity to watch the masque for several hours.

After walking to the site location, with his sidearm attached to his belt to protect against any lone-wolf attack, Harold found a safe vantage point and started his stakeout. During the day, he spotted Marham walk outside the masque several times. He also saw the Iman talk to a young man who was perhaps an operative.

Marham had hugged the young man, who had olive-colored skin and dark-black hair, then ushered him into the masque. Gatewood sent the picture to Rick Owens to have a facial recognition check done. An hour later, an email came back. The man was Abel Nour, a rising star in the USFF field operative ranks. Harold now knew that something important was about to take place.

He watched the masque until dark, and then turned on the night-vision feature on his binoculars. An hour after darkness arrived, he saw a familiar figure walk out the door of the masque and hug a dark-haired young woman, and then escort her inside.

Harold was not able to get a good look at the woman, as she did not turn around , and walked into the masque with her back toward his line of vision. He remained at his post until ten p.m. when Abdel Nour walked from the masque. He waited another hour for the woman to appear, but she did not. He then returned to his hotel.

Unknown to Gatewood, when the young woman had arrived, Rasul had hugged her and told her he was proud of her, as she was starting to show real progress toward her goal of becoming a first-class USFF agent. The compliment had raised the woman's enthusiasm for the mission, and her commitment to the USFF.

Rasul, Abdel Nour, and the woman had then discussed the mission. Rasul went over the steps of mission, each time stopping and having his two agents tell their actions and responsibilities at that stage. They ten role played the mission, again having the agents tell their duties at each stage of the mission.

When Rasul was confident his two agents were ready for attack, he hugged them and sent them on their journey home, Abdel leaving by the font of the masque, and the woman by the back door, as she was heading in to opposite direction of Nour.

Rasul was overjoyed, as he had trained his agents to the point of perfection, and they were ready. He also was pleased with himself. His conversation with Ala Al-Din, the USFF leader in Damascus, had caused him to reassess his life, and his dedication to Islam and the USFF.

He had undergone a revelation, and had recommitted himself to the goals he had embraced when he had first joined the USFF.Before going to bed,

Rasul had double-checked his supplies for the mission. His bomb materials had been delivered as requested, and the building of the explosive device was completed except for the detonator, which would be completed just before the mission was started.

Rasul had then gone to Iman Marham's quarters and talked with him about the status of the mission, and thanked him for his kind words that had helped him through his personal struggle and his recommitment to the USFF's goals and beliefs.

In his hotel room, Gatewood was pleased, as he had uncovered a team of USFF agents who were about to wage an attack. He had not determined the target yet, but he was on the right track, and would go to work on it in the morning. He had sent his report to Rick Owens and had asked for help in determining the target. Owens had replied, I will put our best analyst, Tayeb Rizwan, on it immediately."

Little did Gatewood know that Rizwan was one of the three moles inside the CIO, and that the correct name of the target would never see the light of day.

Gatewood had then gone to bed, looked at the empty space next to him, and thought about Cindy. He wondered what she was doing, and if she had enjoyed her evening with her parents. He would have much rather had her stay with him tonight, but he understood that her family was important to her, and that they would make up for lost time tomorrow night.

He also did some soul-searching, as he was with Cindy, had two babies on the way and a new life planned with Susana Richards, and had also been thinking about Yua Hayato in Tokyo more and more each day. His life was one of enjoyment, but he wondered if he was walking a tightrope with his emotions at the present time.

Since he had joined the CIO, his life had gravitated toward a state of danger and living in the moment, because he did not know if he would live to see the next moment, as many people now wanted his scalp.

Gatewood then laughed when realized he had used the word scalp. It reminded him of Susana, when she had performed that precision surgical technique on four of his adversaries.

He laughed again when he thought of how he should probably steer clear of Susana because of her jealous and violent personality quirks. But, she had never acted on them with him, as she was totally different when they were together. He thought he knew how to handle her. That ability would soon be put to the test when they were together, with the twins.

He thought, "That is for the future, and I need to live in the present to survive." He then closed his eyes, and was immediately asleep.

Chapter 30

Catching Up

March 6

THE NEXT MORNING, GATEWOOD SLEPT LATE, THEN went through his usual morning routine. He had decided that nothing was likely to happen at the masque until after the noon prayer worship. He would then watch to see if Abdel Nour would reappear. If he did, Harold had decided to follow him.

After taking up his safe viewing position again, Harold waited until two-thirty in the afternoon. When he was almost ready to end the surveillance, Nour exited the front of the masque. Gatewood crossed the street and followed him from a safe distance behind his target.

Abdel walked a zig-zag path through the streets, making left and right turns at the intersections he reached, and then continuing on towards his goal. He had been trained well by the USFF, as the short twelve block distance to his destination, a small grocery store had taken over thirty minutes.

The target had looked over his shoulder, and had stopped to check out the view of the streets behind him, several times. Once at the grocery store, he entered said hello to the owner and a woman employee, had placed a white apron on his body, and had started to stock food, in cans and small bags, on the shelves.

Gatewood watched Abdel work for several minutes from a seat on a bench across the street. He was surprised when both a man who appeared to be the owner, and the woman employee, came up to him, spoke, and then hugged him.

The more Gatewood watched, the more he realized that the grocery store was a family business run by an Islamic-worshiping family. Abdel's name meant, "Servant of the Light." It was obvious to Harold that Nour's commitment to the USFF and Islam was real.

If he was to become Harold's adversary in the mission, he would be a tough, dedicated, worthy, fanatical opponent. Gatewood knew that he must be ready if that circumstance arose.

After another hour of surveillance, Gatewood had decided that he had learned what he had needed for the day, and knowing that Cindy would arrive at the hotel after work, he returned to his room, showered, and waited for her to walk through the door, with a smile on her face. He had not known that he had not been the only person following someone today, as he himself had been followed, and his every move had been monitored.

He was not disappointed when Cindy turned the key and entered the room, with a smile from ear-to-ear on her face. She closed the door, peeled off her blouse, then the rest of her clothing, throwing them to the right, and then to the left, and giggling as clothing landed on the rug. She then walked, nude, to Harold, kissed him, and led him to the bed.

She removed his clothes, pulled back the covers, slid onto the sheets, reached out, took Harold's hand, and pulled him onto the bed. She said, "I have missed you.", and proceeded to kiss him from head to toe. They made love for over an hour, and then talked as she laid in his arms.

"Harold, when I am with you, I am the happiest I have ever been in my life. When I am away from you, I am the most miserable as I have ever been in my life. I don't want you to ever leave me. I wish we could be together forever."

"I feel the same type of love for you too Cindy."

"I wish I did not have to stay in London, with my family."

"You don't have to stay. You can go anywhere you want."

"No, my parents are very controlling and possessive. They expect me to live here the rest of my life."

"They love you, and they want the best for you. That is why they don't want you to leave."

"I want to stay right here, beside you for the rest of my life."

Harold kissed her, and said, "Maybe that will happen Cindy."

Chapter 31

Go…

March 7

CINDY TURNED OVER, LOOKED AT HAROLD KISSED him softly on the lips, and said good morning. Harold smiled and said, "You were magnificent last night. You outdid yourself. You wore me out."

She smiled and said, "Harold, if anything ever happens to me, I want you to know how much I love you."

He replied, "I love you too. But, what could happen to you?"

"I could die."

"That is not going to happen for a very long time Cindy."

She said, "I hope not."

The couple then made love, showered together, and Cindy left for work. Her comments had forced Harold to think that something terrible was bothering her, and he decided to follow her to find out what had caused her strange behavior. She walked in an opposite direction from her workplace, toward the train station.

She bought a ticket on the ten o'clock train from London to Liverpool, and sat down in the terminal, scanning the people who were seated on the long, decades-old benches. She suddenly stood up and walked toward a man who had his back facing toward her, who was reading a magazine at the newsstand inside the terminal. She stopped beside him, spoke to him while staring straight ahead, then turned and walked to the boarding area for the Liverpool train.

The man then walked after her, toward the same destination. He stopped by her side when he reached her, spoke, and then turned his head to see if they were being watched. The man was Abdel Nour.

Gatewood was speechless. What was Cindy doing with him? He continued to watch the two people, his mind a whirling blob of confusion. A third man approached them, spoke, and then boarded the train. Cindy and Abdel followed suit, and boarded the train.

Gatewood rushed to the ticket window where Cindy had bought her ticket, and bought one for himself. He then rushed to the train, boarded just as the conductor was about to grab the step that allowed easier, safer access to the train, and entered one of the railcars.

He searched one car, then another. He looked through the window of the third car, and saw all three of the people he was tailing.

They were talking, apparently about something important, as Rasul was pointing in one direction, and had tapped Abdel Nour on his knee, and had motioned for him to head forward, toward the baggage car. Rasul handed Abdel a large gym-style bag, and Abdel then moved toward his destination.

Rasul closed his eyes, pulled his hat over his eyes, stretched out in his seat, and appeared to head toward slumber land. Cindy was facing the window, looking out at the city as the train pulled away from the station.

Gatewood slipped past the now-sleeping Rasul, and Cindy, who had now closed her eyes and was still facing the window. Gatewood made his way through the passenger cars, looking for Nour.

Harold reached the baggage car, looked through the window, and saw Abdel kneeling, setting the timing device on a powerful bomb that would explode, derail the train, and cause many deaths.

He took his pistol from its holster under his shirt, and entered the baggage car. He yelled, "That's enough Abdel. Put everything down." Nour laughed, stood up, and stated to point his weapon at Harold. He yelled. "I am on a mission and Allah will not be denied."

Gatewood said, "Not today", and fired three shots into the Abdel's chest cavity. Gatewood then moved to the bomb to disarm it. Before he could do so, another person entered the railcar, their weapon drawn and pointed at Harold.

A voice said, "Stop Harold."

Gatewood looked up, then said, "Gianna, what are you doing here?"

"I am on a mission for the OWFA. I do not want to kill you Harold, because I love you. But, we must leave the train. The OWFA wants the bomb to detonate, and to have you go up with it, but I will not let that happen. Come with me."

Before Harold could answer, Halim Rasul entered the baggage car, pushed Gianna Sabina to the floor, and told Gatewood to put his weapon on the floor in front of him. Cindy Almas followed Rasul into the car, her weapon drawn, and walked to Gatewood's left, then stopped.

Gatewood said, "Cindy, how could you?"

Rasul spoke before Cindy could explain her situation to Harold. "Her real name is Cindy Nour. Her parents are Syrians who have now settled in London.'

Harold looked at Cindy and said, "That explains your olive-colored skin."

Cindy's facial expression had changed, as her eyes were now misty with tears. She said, "I love you, but you killed my brother."

Rasul had turned his head toward Cindy when she had spoken. Gatewood lid to the floor, grabbed his gun, shot, and killed Rasul with a bullet to his heart.

Gianna then raised her weapon toward Cindy. Before she could fire, Cindy shot her in the stomach. She fell to the floor, and her red blood started to form a pool in front of her.

Cindy then pointed her pistol at Harold, and said, "I love you Harold, but I must do this to honor my brother Abdel and my parents." As she started to squeeze the trigger, a bullet blasted through her forehead, and her pretty little face exploded with blood. She dropped to the floor, dead on arrival.

Gatewood looked toward Gianna. She had slumped to the floor, her weapon had slid from her hand, and she had entered death's arms.

Harold then scrambled to the bomb, found the kill switch, and deactivated the device. He then sat down. Leaned against the suitcases and bags behind him and surveyed the scene.

Beside him, on the right, laid Abdel Nour, dead from the three rounds Harold had pumped into his chest. In front of him, Halim Rasul was stretched out on the floor, and had joined the other USFF agents Gatewood had sent to hell. Harold laughed and said, "Good riddance."

To his right, ten feet away, Gianna Sabina, his beautiful mistress from his mission in Rome, laid in a pool of her own blood, dead, but freed from any further missions for the OWFA, after being shot by Cindy Nour.. Harold said, "She was beautiful, and luckily for me, she was too tender-hearted to be a killer. She saved my life, as the cost of her own."

To his left, aka Cindy Almas, in reality Cindy Nour, laid dead, shot by Gianna, who she had then shot herself. Harold said, "She was a beautiful woman. If circumstances had been different we might have had a future together."

Harold looked at the carnage around him, and said, "I want to go home, and be with Susana and the two babies who are on the way. That is where my life is now. I want to be done with the spy business. My life has taken an important new direction, and I want to enjoy it to the fullest with Susana and the babies. We will have many wonderful years together. It will be perfect."

Chapter 32

D.C.

March 8

AFTER CALLING RICK OWENS AND TELLING Him what had happened on the train from London to Liverpool, Harold was cleared of any charges, and taken back to his hotel. Tomorrow, he would fly to Washington, D. C. to talk with Owens and Robbins, and then his shrink, Dr. Charles Long.

In his room, Harold ordered a large salad, strawberries and blueberries, and to celebrate, a pitcher of lemonade. He hoped that the drink would be as good as the lemonade his mother had fixed him when he was a boy. He longed for that taste, as he had not enjoyed it for a very long, long time.

He then headed to the bathroom. He was exhausted, and took a long, hot shower, the beads of water penetrating into the pores of his battered, sore body. He wanted to stay in the shower for hours, to wash away his soreness, and to cleanse his mind of the horrors he witnessed in the train's baggage car. He closed his eyes and relaxed.

In the hallway, a man approached his door, perhaps with his order from room service. He took a key he had obtained from a maid, and opened the door. He closed the door after entering the room, and hearing the water running in the shower, walked to the bathroom. He entered the room, stopped, and looked at the shower. The shower curtain was drawn to prevent the beads of water from dripping to the floor.

He carried something in his right hand. He reached out with his left hand and jerked the shower curtain open. He cursed, as no one was in the shower. He then heard a voice from behind him say, Drop it Iman Tabassum Marham. Don't you know that your actions are not those that a Iman should be doing?"

Tabassum then tried to raise his pistol to the level of Gatewood's chest in an attempt to shoot him. Gatewood fired three rounds into the Iman, causing him to drop, hit his head on the top of the bathtub, then fall to the floor. As blood from his chest ran on to the floor, beads of water sprayed on Marham's body, forming a pink pool on the floor.

Gatewood looked at the dead Iman and said, "No, I guess you didn't know your actions were not worthy of a man of God."

Gatewood walked to the phone near his bed, called the desk and asked for body disposal services. He then sat down on the bed and said, "I am really ready to leave Londinistan."

The next morning, Harold flew to D.C., covered the details of his mission. When they had finished he headed to the airport for his trip home to Gibson City, Illinois.

He entered the terminal and headed to security, so he could be cleared to head to his departure gate. He stopped, answered his cell phone, and then he became pale, unnerved, an upset. He said, "I will be right there."

He changed his destination and headed to see Susana Richards. He arrived, took a cab to see her, and walked through the doors of large building. He then rode the elevator up to the seventh floor, found her room number, and walked to her. She was asleep, lying on her back. He bent down and kissed her, which caused her to open her eyes.

She started to sob, and Harold wiped away the tears from her cheeks. She finally quit crying and out her hands around his neck, and drew him closer to her.

"Harold, I am so sorry. I had a miscarriage and lost both babies."

Harold kissed her softly on the lips and asked how she was feeling. She said she was very tired and that the doctors had told her that her condition was serious. She then said, "Harold, I love you.'

Gatewood answered, "I love you too Susana. You are going to be alright. We will try again to have children." She then closed her eyes, and Harold sat down on a chair near the bed. He then softly said, "We will try again Honey. We will try again."

Printed by Libri Plureos GmbH in Hamburg, Germany